HERS TO CLAIM

The Nightstar Shifters 4

———————————————

ARIEL MARIE

It will always be you, for the rest of my life and beyond.

Unknown

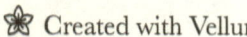 Created with Vellum

CHAPTER ONE

"You are going through with this mating and that's final!" Rovel Norden shouted.

Echo paused, staring at her father. It was rare for the large bear shifter to raise his voice at his only daughter. She bit back a scream of frustration. Tears blurred her vision. She blinked, refusing to cry in front of him.

Thirty-one years of life, and he had always given her what she wanted. As the youngest offspring, she had been the spoiled one. Her elder brothers, Vick and Cole, continuously teased her because she would get away with murder when it came to their father.

"But, Dad, it's not fair. Why are you not imposing this on Vick or Cole? They are older than me." She ran a hand through her dark hair and walked away from him. She tried to push down her emotions, but she couldn't. She moved to the window of the family room and gazed out at the thick forest that lined their property.

"I've already spoken with your brothers, and they are on board. I'll be looking for their matches, too."

Echo closed her eyes and inhaled. So, all three Norden children would be forced into arranged matings.

If her mother were alive, she wouldn't allow this. Zottie Norden had a way about her that always calmed her mate down.

She wouldn't stand for her children being matched off.

"What happened to allowing fate to guide us?" Echo shuddered at the thought of her intended mate.

Hyde Gillian.

He belonged to their clan. They had grown up

together, and he had made her life a living hell when they were cubs.

Echo had always been a thick girl. Her mother had told her she was just big boned. But Echo knew there was no such thing.

She was a bear shifter who loved to eat. She was curvy in all the right places. She'd always been chased by men and women. Everyone wanted a good snuggle buddy, especially when it grew chilled. Here in Southern California, the temperature could drop to around fifty, and that's when she'd have suitors sniffing around her.

That's why she was currently single. Just when she thought she had met a decent person, they showed their true colors.

"I've been waiting for you and fate to come to a decision," her father snapped. His tone softened. "Echo, baby. You know I just want what is best for you. You aren't getting any younger."

"Thanks for reminding me that I'm getting older," she grumbled. She glanced over her shoulder at him. He suddenly looked every one of his sixty-five years. Thanks to shifter genes, he stopped aging when he hit fifty. "Just give me more time. What about if I'm not mated by thirty-five, then we can—"

"What is done, is done," he interjected.

Echo's shoulders slumped at the announcement.

"You will be mated to Hyde. I know you don't like him, but he will grow on you. His family is a strong one, and your cubs will help shape the future of this clan."

"So, I'm only good enough to breed the future?" She spun around and faced him. Anger reared its ugly self. Her bear paced back and forth inside her. She was pissed off, too. Of all people they could have been paired up with, it just had to be Hyde. "Continue the family name and all that jazz, but did anyone care to think of what I wanted?"

"You have a duty to your kind," he growled.

His eyes darkened to almost black. His animal was near the surface. He stalked across the room toward her. She backed up until she hit the wall. She wasn't afraid of him or his animal. Neither of them would harm her.

But she knew one thing.

She had pushed Rovel Norden too far.

He was an upstanding member of their town. He was on the alpha's council. The alpha was her father's elder brother. It was no wonder the Gillian family had agreed to the pairing.

Hyde mating with Echo, he would gain status amongst shifters.

Her family was a well-to-do member of the shifter community. The Brokenclaw Clan had settled in Howling Valley not too long after it was founded by the Gerwulf wolf pack. The two shifter communities lived together in harmony.

The bears mostly stayed up in the hills and mountainous region of Howling Valley.

"But, Dad," she tried to interrupt, but he raised a hand to cut her off.

"Finding your one true mate would be hard. We need you to do this, Echo. We need to ensure our new generation is in the works. We have to do our part to ensure bears continue to thrive."

She glanced down at her feet. It was common knowledge that bear numbers were on the decline.

The Brokenclaw Clan had a law.

Bears were to mate with bears.

The number of bear matings were down due to this rule, but Echo wasn't going to be the one voice that aloud.

But what if her fated mate wasn't a bear?

She glanced up and sighed.

A look of regret was on his face. He pushed a hand through his hair that was just as dark as hers.

"If your mother was alive, she'd probably have me strung up a tree for forcing a mating on you, but we have no other choice." He reached out and rested his large hand on her shoulder. "Tonight will be the engagement party."

"What?" Echo gasped. "Why are we rushing this? You just told me today you agreed to a pairing and already there's a party?"

She brushed past him, unable to catch her breath. Panic took over Echo. Her bear was demanding to be let out.

Mating.

Engagement party.

Hyde.

This was all too much.

She took off running through the house, ignoring his shout. She burst out of the back door and headed toward the forest. Fur erupted out of her skin and traveled up her body.

Echo allowed the change.

Her bear burst forth, her clothes falling to the ground in tattered shreds. A snarl escaped her mouth as she sped away.

Her bear was just as pissed off as she was. She headed into dense woods at full pace. The animals of the wild scattered, not wanting her to set her sights on them.

No one would dare mess with an angry grizzly.

Echo continued on until she grew tired. She had lost track of time and how far she had gone. The thick trees had thinned out, revealing a creek.

Echo recognized the area. It was somewhere she would come when she wanted to get away. It was a few miles from her father's house and not too far from her cabin.

She walked over to the water and took a long drink. Her bear was exhausted. It had been a while since she had run that far.

Not that she was lazy, Echo just preferred not to run unless she had to.

She took another sip of the cool water and sighed. Sitting on the bank, she tried to understand her father's point of view. Echo couldn't

There was no way in the seven hells she would ever force her child to mate with someone they didn't like.

Her bear snorted.

Saying she didn't like Hyde was being nice.

She despised him.

He was always rude to her and obnoxious.

Her father could have at least found another bear to pair her up with.

Echo took the reins and shifted. Her animal gave her pushback at first, but Echo was the stronger of the two.

"I promise I'll let you back out." She stood from the ground and glanced around. She only sensed a few harmless animals who were nearby, watching her. She smiled, wishing she could be at peace like they were. A deer paused near the edge of the tree line. It dove back into the woods, apparently sensing her animal.

Her bear growled, wanting to run after the doe.

"Not today." Echo waded into the water. She had to think of ways to get out of the arrangement. What if Hyde was the one to back out of the deal?

She came up to her knees.

She knew automatically that Hyde wouldn't back out of hitching himself to her family name.

Echo tilted her head back and stared at the sky.

"Fate, where are you? Where's my mate?" She blew out a deep breath and pushed down the tears that threatened. "I need you to reveal my mate to me. I've always had my complete faith in you. Don't let me down."

"You're telling me the Brokenclaw Clan still believes in something as archaic as arranged matings?" Mindi gasped. She glanced over at her father in disbelief.

Mick Martin, the beta of the Nightstar Pack, was a large man who was quiet, but a powerful wolf. He had helped lead their pack since the alpha took over. He and Evan Gerwulf were close friends having grown up together.

"Yeah, they do." He shrugged. "They want to keep their numbers up, and if they are to do that, then they will arrange matings."

"I mean, I've heard of mating out of convenience, but at least the two people will agree to it." Mindi shook her head and turned toward the window.

Her father was invited to the engagement party. He was obligated to go due to his status in the Nightstar Pack. It was considered a courtesy for them to show.

Mindi couldn't fathom her parents trying to tell her who she should mate with. Her parents may have recommendations of someone who would be a strong match, but they wouldn't force anything on her.

Her family was a close-knit bunch. Mindi was the youngest of three children. Her elder brother, Dirk, and her sister, Luna, were still single as well as she was. Thankfully being shifters, they were able to enjoy long lives and were still considered young.

Her brother was in search of his mate. He was determined to find that person to continue on his name. Luna couldn't care less about finding anyone. She was having too much fun.

Mindi felt that when fate presented the person for her, then she'd react. She, like her sister, was having a blast being single. At the age of twenty-seven, she had plenty of years to settle down and have pups.

At the moment, she had a great life, and finding a mate was not in her plans.

"Why haven't you and Mom pushed us to mate?" Mindi asked.

"One, we believe in fate. She will show you who is meant for you when she is good and ready. Your mother and I were destined to be together. I wasn't even thinking of settling down when I met Adele." A grin appeared on his face.

Mindi groaned, not wanting to imagine a younger version of her parents getting together.

They drove in a comfortable silence up the winding road into the hills. The Brokenclaw Clan preferred the hills and mountains. Howling Valley was a beautiful area made of valleys, hills, and mountains. It was a perfect area for shifters who could blend in with nature.

Their town was a mixed one of humans and paranormal. It was founded on the principle of living together in harmony.

Mindi loved Howling Valley. She had a studio at the edge of town. She was a self-taught photographer and made a good living off of her artwork. She had plenty of inspiration right at her fingertips.

Lately she had expanded in photo shoots of families and individuals. She especially loved her boudoir shoots. Those had become popular with people wanting to dive into their sexuality but keeping it tasteful.

She was becoming a household name. Her clientele was growing at a rapid rate, and she was loving it. Her waitlist for private shoots was booked out six months.

Her hands were itching to snap some photos. She'd brought one of her cameras just in case she could slip out of the party. Her nature photos always sold well online, and the weather was behaving. Nighttime shots would be perfect.

Mindi planned to mingle for a short while, then she was going to escape and grab her camera. She'd be a fool to pass up this beauty of nature at night.

They pulled onto a road and soon were parking outside a large cabin. There were plenty of cars out front with people milling around.

Mindi's wolf sat up, curious.

What is it?

Her wolf stood and paced slowly. Her beast didn't say a word, but something was definitely odd.

Mindi frowned. She didn't sense any danger or anything strange here. She decided to push this weird feeling down and wait for her wolf to let her know what was wrong.

"I'm sure you are wanting to snap some photos. Give me thirty to forty minutes before you disappear." Her father grinned at her.

She burst out laughing. Mick Martin knew her too well.

"Okay." She opened the truck's door and hopped down.

Her father met her in front of the vehicle and

patted her on the back. They strolled toward the house.

"I saw the way you were staring out the window." He chuckled. "Let's congratulate the new couple and mingle. Evan wants me to speak with Trion about something important. That's when you can pull your disappearing act."

Mindi's curiosity was piqued. Why would her father need to speak to the alpha of the bear clan? She should have known there would be a real agenda for attending this party.

CHAPTER TWO

"Congratulations."

Echo smiled and nodded to a member of her clan. She was tired of hearing the word, tired of smiling, and tired of acting as if she was okay with this forced mating.

Almost the entire clan had come for the party.

Echo kept her fake smile plastered on her face. She wore a black dress that was one of her favorites. The only thing was, this damn waist trainer she had put on was making it harder for her to breathe. She had seen an ad for it online and purchased it as a last-minute impulse buy.

Now she regretted the purchase and the fact she had put it on. She wanted to make sure the dress appeared smooth on her body and that everything wasn't jiggling that shouldn't be.

Normally she didn't care, but since the entire clan was coming and would be staring at her, she wanted to look her best.

Not that she really cared what they thought of her, but she wasn't going to be caught in anything less than gorgeous.

Apparently, what they say is true.

Beauty is pain.

Echo walked through her father's home and tried to remain calm. Hyde was off in the corner speaking with a bunch of men, being loud and obnoxious as always.

For the millionth time she had to ask: Why him? He had teased her as a child so much, why would the fates allow her father to match her with him?

Kids could be cruel, and they had been with her. She had always been the plump one in the group, and Hyde had always been the person to point it out.

Echo walked past a mirror and glanced at herself. She looked damned good, and if no one else saw it, she did.

Her bear growled her agreement.

Echo may not be as tall as other female bears with their toned physiques, but it didn't mean she was any less of a bear.

Her little black dress highlighted her body nicely. Her boobs were large and perky, her waist was narrowed, thanks to the trainer, and the material stopped mid-thigh, showing off her generous thighs and well-defined calves.

She'd kept her thick hair down, and her makeup was flawless.

"There she is," her uncle's voice boomed.

Echo turned around and caught sight of Trion walking toward her.

Her uncle and father were of similar build and looks. They could be mistaken for twins, but her uncle was older than her father by two years. The brothers were close when growing up; Echo always thought of her uncle as a second father. When her mom passed away, her uncle and his mate ensured she, and her siblings, were cared for while her father grieved.

"Uncle." She grinned and dove into his open arms.

He wrapped her up tight in his embrace and pressed a kiss to the top of her head.

"You are beautiful as usual," Trion said, stepping back. There was that twinkle in his eye, revealing he was up to mischief. Her uncle was a strong bear who was highly respected and even feared. But when it came to family, he could be a pushover.

"We need to talk," she grumbled. She poked him in the chest. No one else would dare try that with the alpha, but Trion had a soft spot when it came to her and his daughter. They were the only two girls, and both had him wrapped around their little finger.

"I know you aren't happy." His voice lowered. He kept an arm around her shoulder and guided her over toward where her father stood around talking with some of the council members. "But just know that our family's future is in your hands. You will be well rewarded, niece."

"Of all people? You know Hyde teased me unmercifully as a child," she whispered fiercely.

"I know, and he will grovel now at your feet, but his family is a strong one. The match is solid." His smile disappeared, and a hardened glint appeared in his eyes. "Don't worry, niece. All will be well. You and Dari will be well-rewarded for this. I have something in mind."

"You're going to arrange Dari's mating, too?" Echo's cousin, Dari, would not sit idly by to let her father pull something like this. She was just as head-strong as him. Dari and Echo were as close as sisters, and Echo just realized her dear cousin was nowhere to be seen.

"She'll come around it. I know my daughter is a spitfire." Trion squeezed her shoulder.

"Here's my mate-to-be," Hyde's voice appeared at her side. He took her by the arm and winked at her uncle. "Can I borrow her for a moment?"

"Of course you can." Trion nodded to Hyde then glanced at her. "We'll talk later, niece."

"What do you want?" Echo snapped.

"Is that any way to speak to your betrothed?" Hyde laughed.

Her bear rumbled in her chest. She had a few more choice words for him, but she bit her lip to keep from causing a scene.

He guided her over to the group of people he had been speaking with. "I want to introduce you to some friends."

Echo stiffened when he placed an arm around her waist. Her skin crawled from being so close to him. How the hell were they supposed to mate when she grew nauseated just by being near him?

Hyde would be considered handsome by most standards. He was tall and burly like most bear shifter males. He had dark-blond hair, clear blue eyes, with perfect teeth when he smiled.

She glanced over at him, and yup, the nausea was still there.

To mate was forever, and being tied to his man was going to be a life sentence.

"Fellas, I would like to introduce you to Echo Norden, the alpha's niece," Hyde announced as they stopped in front of his friends. The alpha's niece? That's how she's introduced?

It took everything for her not to roll her eyes.

"Hello." She put back on her fake smile and nodded to the men in front of her.

"Echo, this is Ward, Conrad, and Barret." Hyde motioned to each of them.

Echo grew uncomfortable under their gazes.

"She's a pretty one. How'd you luck up?" Ward practically licked his chops while he stared at her.

She wanted to walk away, but Hyde's hand tightened on her as if he suspected what she was thinking.

"We've known each other since we were cubs. Isn't that right?" Hyde grinned.

"You mean when we were kids and you called

me Echo the chubster?" Echo turned toward him with her eyebrows raised.

"We were kids then." Hyde waved a hand.

"I always did prefer my women thick." Conrad snorted. He folded his arms in front of his chest and winked at her. "If you change your mind about Hyde, just know I've never had a problem with thick women."

Echo prayed the floor would open up and swallow her whole.

"Get your own mate," Hyde retorted. He tugged Echo to him, closing the small gap between them. "Echo will come around."

Echo rolled her eyes. Hyde either didn't see her or didn't care.

"And she has the perfect pair of birthing hips. I can't wait to plant my babies in her. We'll have at least four cubs." He and his friends shared a good laugh.

That was the last straw.

Birthing hips? Were they living in the sixteenth century? Who said things like that?

"I'm parched. I'm going to get a drink." She pulled herself from Hyde's grasp and walked away.

"What did I say?"

Hyde's laughter made her skin crawl again. She

needed to put some distance between them before she did something she would regret.

Echo quickly made her way over to the bar and grabbed the bottle of tequila off the top shelf. The bartender her father hired didn't say a word. The guy handed her a good-sized glass.

"You look like you need this." He chuckled.

"Thanks." She poured herself a hefty drink then handed him back the bottle. She turned around and took a sip and prayed for sanity.

"Echo!"

She inhaled sharply. Her father was calling her name. She opened her eyes and glanced in the direction of his voice. He was standing with a tall man and a woman. Echo's gaze landed on the woman. She had similar features to the man in deep conversation with her father.

Echo's father waved for her to come over. Echo took another sip of her drink and began maneuvering through the crowd.

Echo grew closer to her father, and her eyes met the woman who was staring at her.

Her bear stood up to attention and rumbled deep in her chest.

The woman's amber eyes were glowing.

Wolf shifters.

Echo's bear slammed into her chest.

Mate.

Echo stumbled slightly at the force of her animal. She bumped into one of the elders who was passing her.

"Excuse me," Echo said automatically, not paying attention to who she'd almost knocked down to the floor.

"I hope you aren't too far into your cups," Rovel joked when she arrived at his side.

She sheepishly smiled at him. The wolf hadn't taken her eyes off Echo yet.

"I tripped on something," she said. She motioned to her glass. "This is my first one."

Echo cleared her throat, completely shocked at what her bear growled.

It couldn't be.

Was this woman her mate?

"It doesn't matter. This celebration is in your honor." Her father wrapped an arm around her shoulder and squeezed. "Echo, allow me to introduce you to Mick Martin, the beta to the Nightstar Pack, and this is his daughter, Mindi."

Echo smiled and shifted her glass to her other hand. She reached out and took Mick's hand.

"Hello, sir. We've met before." Mick's hand swallowed hers. His grip was strong and warm.

"I thought so. You do look familiar." Mick grinned. He motioned to his daughter. "This is Mindi, my daughter. Not sure if you two have met before."

Echo shook her head. She would have remembered Mindi if they had. Echo reached over and took Mindi's hand in hers.

The electrical current that raced up her arm confirmed all she needed to know.

Mindi was her mate.

CHAPTER THREE

Mindi would never understand the notion behind arranged matings. She observed the people milling around in the home. Everyone was happy and enjoying themselves.

What was so wrong about waiting for fate?

Or at least a couple agreeing to a mating of convenience.

"And she has the perfect pair of birthing hips."

Mindi's head snapped around to the deep voice across the room. Her shifter hearing picked up on that conversation. What the hell was that supposed to mean?

She glanced over at the asshole and shook her head. He was a huge bear of a man, who apparently was drinking and just being rude. Her gaze landed on the voluptuous woman standing next to him, and she no longer paid any attention to him. She didn't look too pleased with the guy.

Mindi's wolf stood. She pawed at Mindi's abdomen. Her wolf was interested in the gorgeous brunette.

Who wouldn't be? She was a total knockout.

The woman he had been talking about stalked away and headed to the bar.

She was a curvy thing who definitely piqued Mindi's attention. The swell of her hips and the sway in her walk had Mindi's wolf standing at attention.

Mindi had promised her father to stick around for a little. She was glad her father wasn't pressuring her into mating. She wasn't interested in settling down yet. She had a good life, a successful business, and plenty of women she could call on if she was needing a soft body to warm her bed.

She loved women, and every single one she was involved with knew she didn't want any strings attached. Everything was for good ol' fun.

People had eyed her and her father when they'd

first arrived. They were the only wolves in attendance. She was sure everyone was curious as to why they were there, but it was all some political crap Mindi didn't want to have anything to do with.

"Where are my manners? Mindi, this is Rovel, the alpha's brother." Mick did the late introductions.

"Pleased to meet you." Mindi smiled and shook Rovel's hand. "This is one heck of a party."

"Thank you. My daughter, Echo, is the lucky girl." Rovel chuckled.

Was she lucky? The poor girl was probably forced into this archaic tradition.

"Where is she?" Mick asked.

"Echo!" Rovel shouted.

The curvy woman at the bar turned around with a drink in her hand. He motioned for her to join them.

Mindi's wolf paced while Echo made her way to them.

Mate.

Mindi froze in place, unable to tear her eyes from Echo. What the hell did her wolf just say?

Oh no. We're not doing that. We have a good life.

Her wolf growled and continued pacing. Obviously, her animal didn't agree with her.

Echo drew closer to them, and it was then Mindi was able to see how beautiful the woman truly was. The air escaped Mindi's lungs. She was enraptured with Echo.

Even her name was sexy.

Echo arrived next to her father. Mindi didn't hear a thing that was said. Her wolf was now howling inside.

This was her mate.

Echo held her hand out to Mindi. They shook hands, and a jolt of electricity raced up her arm.

Mindi cleared her throat and was finally able to find her voice. "How are you?"

"As good as can be under the circumstances." Echo laughed.

Mindi's core clenched at the sound.

"Echo, Mindi is a photographer. Maybe we can book her for the mating ceremony?" Rovel suggested.

Echo's eyes widened.

"Wait, are you the photographer who's located downtown?" Echo asked.

"Yup, that's me. I can check my calendar and see what I can work with." Mindi wasn't too keen on shooting Echo and that asshat. Something about him rubbed Mindi the wrong way, and they had never even spoke.

"I was actually interested in some professional photos for my business. I'm updating my website and would love to speak with you about it." Echo ignored her father's suggestion.

"Sure, we can chat anytime." Mindi nodded.

Echo eyed the room, and a slight look of panic crossed her features.

"Will you excuse me? I need some fresh air." Echo's gaze landed on the front door. She practically bolted away from them.

"I'll go with you." Mindi used this as her excuse to get out of the house. She didn't wait for her father's response and followed Echo.

Mindi stepped outside and found Echo standing at the far end of the porch. She leaned against the pillar with her back to Mindi.

Mindi's wolf urged her to go to her. Comfort her. It was obvious Echo was overwhelmed by everything.

"Are you okay?" Mindi asked softly. She approached Echo quietly and stood near her. She breathed in her scent, closing her eyes briefly. The aroma of the woman was like an aphrodisiac.

Honeysuckle with a hint of musk.

She wasn't sure if it was Echo's natural essence or a perfume. Whatever it was, Mindi wanted to get closer and breathe it in.

"Eventually I will be," Echo admitted. She brushed back a wayward strand of her hair from her face. "I'm just overwhelmed by all of this. I didn't find out about the arrangement until this morning."

"What?" Mindi stared at her in shock. That was just downright cruel. To make a plan and not even include the person whose life was the center of the agreement showed they were too busy planning the future.

"Yeah, your face matches how mine was this morning," Echo chuckled. She exhaled and folded her arms in front of her ample chest.

Mindi's attention moved to the mounds, and she licked her lips. The need to see what they looked like grew inside her.

Mindi blinked.

This wasn't the time. Echo was clearly upset, and daydreaming of stripping the woman out of her dress would not help her at the moment.

Laughter filled the air along with music. Echo cringed, then sniffed.

Mindi's wolf urged her to do something.

"Why don't you go for a walk? Getting away from everything may help calm you down."

Echo glanced over at her. Her dark-brown eyes were big, and even in the low light, Mindi could see the small flecks of gold.

"Will you come with me?" Echo asked softly. She studied Mindi. Worry flashed in her eyes as if she expected Mindi to decline the invitation.

Mindi had a soft spot for beautiful women.

One as sexy as Echo, she would follow anywhere.

"Yeah, of course." Mindi smiled at her.

They walked down the few stairs and headed toward a path that led into the woods.

They fell into a comfortable silence and made their way from the house. Mindi kept stealing glances at the woman. She was beautiful, and Mindi was at a loss on why the girl wasn't in a relationship with someone instead of having to be arranged in one.

Had Echo been a wolf shifter, she would have had suitors beating down her door.

Her wolf growled at the thought of someone pursuing Echo.

They strolled deeper into the forest. Mindi's

wolf grew excited they had her alone. She wanted to get to the know the curvy bear shifter.

Mate.

Her wolf kept repeating the word.

Mindi tried to shut her animal up, but the stubborn beast was determined to convince Mindi otherwise.

Maybe her animal was wrong. Echo was beautiful and voluptuous, and maybe having sex with her would quiet her wolf.

The thing that worried Mindi was the fact her wolf had never considered any other woman before Echo to be her mate.

Why now?

The woods were beautiful, and the dark sky was littered with tiny stars. Her photogenic eye was capturing so many beautiful parts of the woods that it left her dying to go grab her camera from the truck.

But she would wait.

Echo needed her.

"Can I ask why you agreed to the matching. I can clearly see you don't want it," Mindi asked. She couldn't help it. She was curious by nature and needed to know the answer.

"I wasn't really given much choice." Echo

shrugged. "It's getting harder for bears to find their mates. We need to have offspring so we can continue to thrive. According to my father and my uncle, it's my duty to my kind."

"I find it hard that bears can't find their mates. I swear everyone in my pack has been tripping over their mates lately." Mindi snorted. She thought of all of the pairings being announced. The most recent couple was Addy and Cora. Addy, a member of the Nightstar Pack, had fallen in love with the new witch in town.

"Really? Are you, um, mated?" Echo glanced over at Mindi. She almost appeared shy when she asked the question.

"Nope, and don't plan on getting mated yet either." Mindi had to force those words out. Her wolf snarled at her. She was trying to ignore her animal who was now pacing inside her.

"Do you ever want to find your mate?"

Mindi thought about it. Did she want to find her mate?

Sure.

Just now wasn't in the cards for her. She was living her best life, and with her business taking off the way it was, she may not be able to have time for a mate.

"I do. I'm young and still want to travel and have fun." Mindy giggled.

Echo grimaced, and Mindi's smile disappeared. She paused, automatically reaching for Echo. Was she in pain? They had put a good amount of distance between them and the party. The sound of music was faint.

"Are you okay?"

"Yeah, it's just this damn waist trainer." Echo rubbed her stomach.

"A what?" Mindi was taken aback. Why would Echo put herself in such a contraption?

"You know, a girdle. To hold all of this in." Echo motioned to her stomach.

Mindi closed the gap between them. Her eyes were locked on Echo's midriff. She was beautiful and shouldn't have to hide any part of her body.

"Why would you try to alter perfection?"

Echo was frozen in place. Their breasts brushed against each other with every breath they took.

"What are you doing?" Echo asked.

Mindi lifted Echo's dress. The heat radiating

from the wolf's eyes was breathtaking. Her amber eyes were glowing, her beast near the surface.

Echo's bear recognized Mindi's beast and roared.

The big grizzly headbutted Echo, demanding to be released.

Mindi's hands slid up Echo's thighs and over onto the top of the waist trainer that covered Echo's stomach.

"I'm freeing you." Mindi smirked. Her fingers flew over the tiny hooks and began undoing them. "You don't need this."

"I don't?" Echo whispered. Mindi's lips were close enough that if Echo moved a hairsbreadth their lips would meet.

"No, you don't."

Mindi finished what she was doing, and Echo immediately felt relief when Mindi removed the trainer from around her. A sigh escaped Echo. The pleasure that filled her once she wasn't being contained was heavenly.

"Goddess, that feels wonderful." Echo moaned. Her eyes fluttered shut for a moment before opening.

Mindi stared at her, lust evident on her face.

Mindi tossed the trainer into the bushes. She reached up and cupped Echo's face.

"I would love to photograph you," Mindi murmured. Her hands made their way to her hair and pushed it back, tucking it behind Echo's ear. Her other hand was still resting on Echo's bare waist underneath her dress.

"Really?"

"Yes," Mindi hissed.

Their lips merged in a kiss. Echo wasn't sure who kissed who first, but all she knew was that she was loving it.

Mindi's warm lips moved across hers in a soft steady rhythm. Echo parted her lips, inviting Mindi's tongue inside.

Echo pressed closer to Mindi, her arms coming to wrap themselves around Mindi's neck.

The kiss deepened. Mindi's tongue stroked Echo's.

Echo's heart raced, her body reacting to Mindi. It was going up in flames. The heat consumed her body as desire raged through her.

Mindi walked her backwards until she was met by a large tree.

"You should never hide any of this." Mindi lips brushed Echo's.

Her hand slipped up to Echo's voluptuous mounds. Echo's breast was larger than Mindi's hand, but the wolf shifter didn't seem to mind. In fact, she reached over and undid the front clasp of Echo's bra and freed her aching breasts. Her amber gaze dropped down as she pushed up Echo's dress.

"This fucking body should be on display."

Echo cried out when Mindi's lips closed around her taut nipple. The wolf shifter suckled at her breast like a starving pup.

"Oh, goddess," Echo breathed. She had never been turned on like she was now. She had just met Mindi, and she wanted to give herself to the woman. Her body craved sexual relief. Her core dripped with her desire.

The scent of their arousal filled the air. Echo could smell Mindi's juices. She bit her lip, wanting to slide her tongue through her folds to get a taste.

"Will you stop by my studio?" Mindi asked. She nipped Echo's bud with her fangs. She palmed Echo's breast with her other hand, pinching the tight bead.

"Yes," Echo sighed.

Mindi grinned. She gathered Echo into her arms and pressed a hard kiss to her mouth. Their kiss immediately exploded. Echo traced her hands over Mindi's body, learning every inch of the wolf shifter. She cupped Mindi's ass, holding her close.

Mindi massaged Echo's bare breasts, then they tore their mouths from each other.

Echo's heavy breathing was audible. Her panties were soaked, and she didn't care that her dress was practically bunched up around her neck. Her body demanded a release, and she didn't care she was supposed to be at her party celebrating her engagement to someone else either.

She wanted Mindi.

Mate.

Her bear roared.

Mindi stepped back away from her, her lust-filled eyes taking all of Echo in.

"No, you should never hide yourself." Her amber eyes met Echo's. "The sweet smell of your pussy is driving my wolf crazy."

"My bear is going crazy from the aroma of yours," Echo admitted. She had never wanted to beg for someone to fuck her until now.

"We have to get back to the party. I'm sure they will be missing you."

"But I'm aching," Echo whimpered. She slid her hands down her stomach and headed to her soaked panties. She leaned back against the tree and spread her legs wide. Her hand slipped underneath the small scrap of material that hid her pussy.

Her fingers were met with a collection of her juices.

"Fuck," Mindi cursed. A low rumble of a growl escaped the wolf.

The heat in her eyes fueled Echo on. She pushed her panties out of the way. The cool air of the night had her nipples hard, but her body was on fire.

There was no other reason for her to be reacting so strongly to Mindi. Just having the woman watching her turned her on.

"I need this to go away." Echo parted her slick folds and explored her throbbing clit. She swiped across it, a moan ripping from her lips. Her eyes closed, she tried to imagine Mindi's hands on her body. She craved the feel of the wolf's lips around her clit and her tongue dipping inside her.

"Keep going, Echo," Mindi growled.

Echo's eyes flew open at the command.

She rubbed her clit in a smooth steady motion. Her body was teetering on the brink of an orgasm, and it wasn't going to take long for her to climax. Her hand was coated in her honey from it pouring from her.

She flicked her clit harder, putting pressure on it.

Mindi had stepped closer, her gaze locked on Echo's hand.

"Come for me, Echo," Mindi commanded.

Echo's body stiffened, her orgasm rushing toward her. She released a silent scream as she fell into oblivion. Her muscles tightened while the waves of her release flowed through her. A warm rush of her sticky substance coated her fingers.

Her breaths were coming fast. She closed her eyes, trying to drag air into her lungs.

A small hand enclosed around Echo's wrist.

Echo opened her eyes to find Mindi lifting her hand to her mouth. She licked the trails of Echo's release from her fingers.

She sucked the fingers into her heated mouth, cleaning them completely.

"Hmmm...so fucking good." Mindi captured Echo's lips in another smoldering kiss. It was over before Echo was ready for it to be. "We have to get you back to the party."

CHAPTER FOUR

"How are we looking out there?" Echo called out from the kitchen. She was in the midst of taking inventory and just remembered her crew was out front running the bakery.

"We're good," Fay replied. "We should be closing in a bit."

"And don't you think about coming up here to help," Zenesha hollered.

Echo laughed. Her crew was amazing and fun to work with. They were an extension of her family.

Echo owned Honey Bear Bakery. She had opened it about five years ago. Once everything was gone, they closed up shop. When this happened, the rest of the day was spent preparing for the next day and working on custom orders.

"Fine. I'll stay back here and do owner stuff," she joked. She went back over to the counter where she stood and stared down at her order form.

No matter how hard she stared at it, she couldn't see it.

Her mind was filled with Mindi Martin.

She couldn't get the wolf off her mind.

After her mind-blowing orgasm in the woods, they had walked back to the party. Mindi had smiled at her, and they had parted ways as if nothing had happened between them.

She hadn't seen the wolf for the rest of the event.

Her dreams since the party had been painfully erotic. She had woken up on the brink of an orgasm every night. Daily masturbating had almost become routine for her.

Snatching up the papers, Echo made her way into her small office and shut the door.

Echo's bear had been restless since then, too.

Did Mindi's wolf not feel the pull?

How could she walk away from Echo so calmly?

Mindi had been affected that night, too. She'd been aroused. Echo scented it.

She breathed in, still trying to remember the delicious fragrance that had filled the air. Echo flopped down in her chair and blew out a deep breath.

She took out her cellphone and opened the internet browser. She was ashamed to admit she had looked Mindi up online. She hadn't learned much about her the other night, so Echo took it upon herself to stalk Mindi from afar.

Biting her lip, she went to Mindi's page on the popular social media app. There were examples of Mindi's work.

Echo browsed some of the photographs and even had a few she would be interested in inquiring about.

Mindi was talented, but it was the other things that Mindi shared online that captivated her.

There were many photos of Mindi with other women.

Out of town, in bars, parties, or out in nature.

Echo could tell the women intimately knew Mindi.

Their eyes said it all.

Jealously reared its green head in her chest.

Was one of the women her current girlfriend? Mindi had said she wasn't mated and that she was young and wanting to have fun.

How young was she? Mindi did another search online and felt relief. Mindi was only four years younger than Echo.

Echo continued browsing through Mindi's photos. She skipped a few of them where Mindi was in an intimate pose with a woman.

A snarl vibrated from Echo's chest. Her bear didn't appreciate the other women hanging on to Mindi.

After studying Mindi's accounts, Echo came to the conclusion that Mindi certainly did enjoy living life. She was well-traveled and loved to have fun.

Echo was confused.

Her bear had felt the attraction between them. The kisses they had shared had rocked Echo to her core.

Echo wasn't ashamed to admit her bear could be one of the laziest around, but even she took notice of the wolf.

But that wasn't supposed to be.

Bear shifters weren't supposed to mingle with other shifters.

At least, that's how she was raised.

Her clan was adamant about one thing.

Bears mated with bears.

Echo knew ultimately it was up to fate, but what if Mindi was truly her mate?

And again, Echo wondered, why didn't Mindi react to the attraction between them? She'd never heard of a one-sided mating amongst shifters.

Doubt pushed jealousy out of the way.

Did Mindi not want to claim Echo? She had always been a confident woman when it came to her looks and size, but now this was her mate.

Everything mattered.

She began to analyze everything from that night. Mindi didn't touch her when she was masturbating in front of her. She had only watched and given commands.

Why didn't she come help, or hell, throw Echo to the ground and have her way with her?

Echo would have let the wolf shifter do whatever, however she wanted to her.

Echo wouldn't know what to do if Mindi were to reject her.

"Okay, Echo. You have work to do," Echo grumbled. She sat her phone down on her desk and tapped a button on her laptop. She had orders to place or there would be no baking and fulfilling clients' orders.

A knock at the door sounded. She glanced up as it opened.

"Here's my mate-to-be." Hyde grinned, leaning against the doorjamb.

"What are you doing here?" She couldn't believe he'd just dropped by her shop. They weren't that close for him to be stopping by whenever he wanted.

"I'm coming to take you out to lunch." His smile faded. He shrugged. "I figured it was necessary, considering the situation we found ourselves in."

She didn't like the way he was staring at her. She looked around, trying to find any excuse not to go with him.

"Oh, well, this is last-minute," she began and picked up her phone. She swiped, trying to appear as if she inspected her calendar. Mindi's social media page was still up. "Can we do another day? I have an appointment with a client about a cake." She stood and grabbed her sweater off the back of her chair and slid it on.

"Oh, well, that's too bad."

"Rain check?"

"Sure." He nodded and followed her through the bakery.

"Hey, guys. Are you still okay up here? I have to go meet a client," she announced to Fay and Zenesha.

"We sure are," Fay replied without batting an eye. She glanced over at Hyde. "It was nice meeting you."

Echo hadn't shared her upcoming mating with Fay and Zenesha. They were both human but had grown up in Howling Valley. They were familiar with the customs of shifters.

"You, too." Hyde trailed behind her out of the bakery. He turned to her, running a hand through his hair. "Why don't we exchange numbers? We have a lot to talk about."

"Like my birthing hips?" she asked. She folded her arms in front of herself.

He cringed and shook his head.

"Look, I had too much to drink. I had just found out about the match, too, and let's just say I pregamed before I got to your father's house."

"Why did you even agree to this? You hated me growing up." Echo grew bold. Why *would* he agree to this? Out of all the women he could have had, she prayed it wasn't just because of her last name.

"This is why we need to go somewhere and talk. On the sidewalk in front of your bakery is not the place." He stuffed his hands into his pockets.

"Fine." They exchanged numbers. "Just text me and I'll check my calendar."

"Great. Let me walk you to your car."

She thought about resisting, but he was a stubborn bear and wouldn't take no for an answer.

"I'm parked right over there." She pointed down the street.

He escorted her to the car. She got in and waved to him. He stood and waited for her to leave. She started the car and pulled out of the spot. She breathed a sigh of relief once she was on the road. She glanced in the rearview mirror and saw him jogging across the street to his truck.

She didn't know where she was going but she began making the trek down the hill.

Before long, she found herself parked outside Mindi's studio.

Butterflies fluttered in her stomach.

What was she doing here?

She glanced down at herself and sighed. She was dressed for work. Not as a sexy siren like she had been the other night.

Black leggings and a t-shirt.

She looked in the mirror and grimaced. She tunneled her hands through her hair, trying to make herself appear decent.

At least she wasn't covered in flour.

"Oh, well. Here goes nothing." Echo stepped out of her car and shut the door. She stared at the building and exhaled.

Apparently, her bear wanted them to come see Mindi.

She headed toward the building and grabbed a hold of the handle before she chickened out and changed her mind.

She'd been thinking nonstop of Mindi.

Echo smiled and figured she would use the excuse of the business.

Who the hell was she kidding? Mindi was a wolf and would smell a lie a mile away.

The bell sounding over the door snagged Mindi's attention. She was leaning over the table studying prints of a photo shoot she had done for a couple. She wasn't expecting anyone, and her assistant had left for the day.

Mindi stood and stretched. She didn't know

how long she had been hunched over the photos. It had been a tiring day of reviewing jobs and sending out completed prints.

Mindi lived in the loft above the studio and couldn't wait to go upstairs and crash.

But first, she had to see who was stopping by.

The strap to her jean overalls slipped down her arm. She pushed it up and walked toward the foyer of her studio to greet. Today she was dressed casual in overalls and a black bralette with her hair pulled up in a bun on top of her head.

The closer she got to the foyer…the scent of a familiar bear hit her before she saw her.

Mindi grinned.

Mate.

Her animal leaped up and strained against Mindi's stomach.

She had hoped Echo would come to visit her.

The bear had filled her thoughts. The taste of her cream still had her licking her lips. It had taken everything she had not to pounce on the woman.

They were attending her engagement party.

Fucking her in the woods while they should have been at the party would have been tacky.

She would at least wait a few days.

Mindi giggled and walked down the hall that

led to the entrance of her building. Her assistant usually sat up front at the counter where customers could come in and browse the displays.

"Echo." Mindi paused in the doorway, watching Echo study a few pictures hanging on the wall.

Echo jumped and spun around. Her big brown eyes widened when her gaze landed on Mindi.

"Um, hi." Echo waved, a shyness coming over her.

Mindi felt the pull to be near her. She tried to fight her wolf who wanted to break free and rush over to the shy bear.

Mindi bit her lip, the memories of Echo's performance rushing to the forefront.

"I'm glad you stopped by."

"You are?" Echo gave a nervous chuckle. "I went for a drive, and somehow I ended up here."

"See, then it was meant for you to come here." Mindi strolled around the counter and stopped in front of Echo. She took in her natural beauty. Echo didn't need any makeup.

"Were you serious when you said you wanted to photograph me?" Echo fidgeted with her hands.

Mindi smirked, an idea forming in her head. It would be the perfect way to show Echo how beautiful she was. Mindi got mixed signals from her. One moment Echo was confident in her looks, but then as soon as someone paid her a compliment, she didn't believe it.

Well, Mindi was the ideal person to prove to Echo how people truly saw her.

"Come here. I want to show you something." Mindi took Echo by the hand and towed her behind her.

"What is it?" Echo giggled.

"We're going to do your photo shoot today," Mindi tossed out over her shoulder. She led Echo to the main room where she did shoots. The room was bright white where she normally had her clients pose.

"What? I'm not dressed or have makeup on." Echo laughed.

"You won't need any."

"I don't know, Mindi. I need to do my hair—"

"You are fine just the way you are."

Mindi could tell the girl was not used to being the center of attention. Echo was a beautiful woman who should be admired by all.

Mindi guided Echo over to the dressing room and motioned for her to go in.

"You can fix your hair in here. No makeup. I'll be right back with something for you to wear."

Echo nodded and entered the room. She turned and stared at Mindi with uncertainty written all across her face.

Mindi grinned and shut the door.

She went back over to where she had her cameras set up. She glanced around and jogged over to her props closet. She pulled a box of large pillows out. She tossed them all on the floor, creating a plush bed for Echo. She softened the lights and finished prepping the area until she was satisfied.

Mindi went into the wardrobe and searched for something for Echo to wear.

"No. No." She went over to the other side and riffled through the clothing hanging up. Her gaze landed on a sheer white material.

It would be perfect to be dropped against Echo's luscious naked body.

Mindi carried the material over to the dressing room and knocked on the door.

"Did you find something?" Echo asked, opening the door.

"I sure did." Mindi handed her the material. "Put this on and drop it around your neck and allow the material to flow down you, like this."

Mindi stepped back and demonstrated how the material should move.

"Are you sure?" Echo's eyes widened even more.

Mindi stepped forward and caressed Echo's soft cheek.

"Trust me."

CHAPTER FIVE

E cho was almost in a full panic. Her pulse pounded in her ears. She brushed her hair until the thick locks shined.

"No makeup?" She stared at herself in the mirror and groaned. Reaching up, she pinched her cheeks until some color appeared.

Why wouldn't Mindi want her to wear makeup? Wasn't this a professional shoot? Makeup would help hide all her imperfections.

Echo peered down at herself with the sheer material resting over her body. It wasn't going to hide anything.

Her dark areolas were completely visible through the transparent drape. It brushed the floor and swirled around her feet.

She might as well be naked.

Stepping back, Echo regarded herself in the mirror and attempted to see what Mindi would see.

She smiled and tried to make a sexy face but ended up looking as if she were pissed off or constipated. She couldn't tell.

A giggle erupted from her.

What was she doing here?

"It's now or never. I can't stay in here forever," Echo muttered. She went over and peeked her head out the door. Soft music played through the overhead speakers. She stepped out and made her way back to the area where she had seen Mindi's camera stands, the white backdrop, and white umbrellas.

Mindi was behind her camera snapping pictures of the large pile of pillows that were situated on the floor. The lights were not as bright as they were when Echo had first arrived.

The mood was calm, relaxing, and sensual.

"I'm ready," Echo announced.

Mindi's head snapped up, and she glanced over her shoulder in Echo's direction. Mindi's sharp intake of breath was the only sound she made.

"You're absolutely gorgeous." Mindi's amber-eyed gaze trailed over Echo's body.

The heat from it was enough to send a tremor of desire shooting through Echo.

"Thank you." Echo fiddled with her hands, unsure what she should be doing.

"I want you to go lie on the pillows." Mindi motioned for her to come to her.

Echo stopped in front of the wolf shifter, her heart still racing.

"This is just an intimate session between me and you. Don't think of anything else."

Echo nodded, swallowing hard.

Just focus on Mindi.

The scent of Mindi reached Echo. It called to her animal, who was pacing, confused on why she hadn't acted on what was between them.

Mindi tucked Echo's hair behind one ear, then moved to adjust the sheer material. The room was chilled slightly, and if she didn't know any better, she had goosebumps on her bare ass.

"That's better," Mindi murmured. She stepped back, apparently satisfied with what she saw. "Okay, now you can go over to the pillows."

Echo moved over to the humungous pile of soft pillows and lay on them. She tried to arrange the material to cover her body.

"Here, let me help you." Mindi jogged over to her and knelt on the floor. She positioned the pillows behind Echo and then adjusted the makeshift dress.

Echo watched Mindi as she darted back to the camera. She leaned forward and snapped one shot.

"Oh," Echo gasped. She gave a nervous laugh. "I wasn't ready."

"That didn't count." Mindi winked at her. "I'm just testing and adjusting. Give me a second."

Echo lay back and waited. The bed of pillows was actually very comfortable. She rested her head on her arm and watched Mindi go over to the white umbrellas and fiddle with them. She turned to her camera.

Echo waited patiently. Mindi was good at what she did, and Echo was sure her pictures would be perfect.

"Okay. This is much better," Mindi muttered. She eyed Echo and smiled. "I want you to just lie back and have fun."

"Easy for you to say," Echo grumbled. The only photos she had taken lately would have been selfies with her cell phone. She had never had professional shots of her before.

She did what she had seen people do on television.

"Wait." Mindi's head popped up. She stared at Echo, taking her camera off the stand. "We need to get you to relax more. You are too stiff."

Echo groaned.

"I'm super nervous," she admitted.

"Well then, we need to make you comfier." Mindi knelt near her and raised the camera, snapping a picture. "The other night, I wanted to lick all the cream from your pussy."

Echo's head snapped around toward Mindi. Her breath caught in her throat at the wolf's admission. One of the things that had bothered her since the other night was Mindi's lack of involvement. Hearing her confession made Echo feel a little better.

Shifters were known for acting on instinct.

Since Mindi had shared something with her, she would do the same.

"I knew your pussy was wet. I scented it and I wanted to taste you as well," Echo admitted.

Mindy snapped another picture.

"Your cream was divine," Mindi purred.

Echo's body was responding to Mindi. She relaxed back against the pillows. The sheer material was gliding across her skin, teasing her. Echo's nipples drew into tight buds.

"I want you to touch yourself again, Echo. Will you do this for me?"

Mindy took another photo.

Echo nodded. Her body was growing warm. It had been cool in the room before, but now it was heating up.

Echo smoothed a hand over the material, tracing her breasts underneath it. She played with her nipple, pinching it.

Her core clenched.

"After that night, I dreamt of you," Echo said. Her breaths were coming faster. She cupped her breasts and massaged them. Her back arched off the pillows as she moved to the rhythm of the music playing in the background.

Images of her dreams came to her. The first one had been innocent with them talking and sharing a kiss, but then as more dreams plagued her, they became more intense and erotic.

Her muscles loosened while her body slid amongst the bedding.

"Tell me about the dreams." Mindi glanced at

her from behind the camera. The whirl of the shutters could faintly be heard.

The covering was irritating Echo. She took the material and pushed it off to the side, leaving her completely naked.

Echo couldn't care less.

Having Mindi watching her fueled her desire and loosened her inhibition.

"In my dreams there was you and me," Echo began. Her legs fell open, giving Mindi a full view of her pussy. Her core clenched with the thought of Mindi touching her. She was falling under the spell Mindi had created by sharing her deep secret. "We were naked, and you were licking my tits."

She picked both of her nipples, eliciting a gasp from her lips. Her hips gyrated, thrusting into the air. Her arousal grew.

"Then what did I do?" Mindi asked, her voice growing husky.

"Trailed kisses from here." Echo tugged on her nipples then released them. Her hands skated along her torso and headed out toward her pussy. "And ended here."

Echo parted her slick folds to reveal her sensitive clit. It was swollen and begging to be suckled.

"And?" Mindi's voice came out strained.

"You fucked me with your fingers." Echo groaned. She pushed two fingers deep inside her slick channel. Her eyes were closed, and her body writhed on the bed of pillows. She became lost in what she was doing.

She opened her eyes and held Mindi's gaze as she finger-fucked herself.

"Is that all I did?" Mindi cleared her throat.

"No," Echo whispered. She slid her other hand between her legs and strummed her clit. "Your tongue flicked my clit at the same time."

Echo cried out. The pleasure rippling through her body was too great. She needed Mindi.

She didn't know how or why the wolf would hold back.

Did she want Echo to beg?

Mindi was losing control. The scent of Echo's juices was overtaking her. She tried to continue taking photos of Echo, but she was getting distracted by the sight of Echo's fingers disappearing into her pussy.

Echo's body was a masterpiece. The coloring of her skin was heightened by her arousal. Her body had softened and fully relaxed back against the pillows.

Her wolf stood and howled.

Mate.

Mindi tried to ignore it, but the aroma of Echo was too tempting.

She moved over to the stand and put her camera back on it. She set the auto-shoot timer for every fifteen seconds. She loved this option for when she wanted to take pictures of herself.

A growl ripped from Mindi. She stalked over to where Echo was, stripping her clothes off. Mindi crawled over to Echo and lay down on her stomach where her face was eye level with Echo's pussy.

Mindi pulled Echo's fingers from her drenched channel. The scent of her was stronger. Mindi moaned, inhaling the tangy scent.

Mindi suckled Echo's fingers clean. She covered her pussy with her mouth. Echo cried out. Mindi sucked in all of her juices that escaped, sending her tongue to dive inside.

Mindi was almost frantic as she consumed Echo. She pushed Echo's thighs apart while she feasted on her. She drank in all of Echo. Her tongue laved the entire length of her from her clit to her anus.

"Mindi!" Echo cried out. Her hips thrust toward Mindi's face. Her hand shot out and gripped Mindi's thick strands.

She latched on to Echo's clit and pulled on it.

Echo chanted her name and rode her tongue. Mindi put her complete focus on Echo's clit.

She was soon rewarded. Echo's muscles tensed, then a scream erupted from her.

Mindi drank in all of Echo's release.

Echo flopped back down on the pillows, her chest rising and falling swiftly. Mindi released her swollen bud and crawled over Echo. She peppered kisses along the way on her stomach and up to her breasts. The full mounds were more than a handful.

Mindi took her time bathing both of them with her tongue. Her pussy dripped with her juices as she consumed all of Echo. She finally moved up higher and took Echo's lips in a bruising kiss.

Mindi rubbed her naked breasts against Echo's. Their nipples rolled on each other. They shifted onto their sides, their limbs entwined with each other.

Their lips were still dancing together in a passionate kiss.

Claim her.

Mindi's wolf growled, pacing back and forth.

The need was growing, and Mindi wasn't sure she would be able to control it.

Echo was promised to another, but that wasn't fate. It was family members meddling in something they had no business poking into.

Echo was meant for Mindi.

Who would have thought, a bear and a wolf?

But the real question was, did she want to really take a mate now?

And did she have a choice?

CHAPTER SIX

E cho moaned softly. She rested back on the soft mattress and the heavenly pillows that were positioned underneath her head. Sometime yesterday afternoon, Echo had taken them upstairs to her loft, the photo shoot completed.

It was a beautiful area with exposed brick on the walls and large windows that allowed natural light to come in. Mindi had tastefully decorated it with neutral colors that contrasted perfectly with the hardness of the brick. Remarkable pictures lined the walls, giving it a homey feel.

It was designed with an open concept in mind.

There was a kitchenette in one corner, a small living area in the other, while Mindi's sleeping area and private bath was located in the back.

Mindi's platform bed was lowered onto the floor. The bedding was comfy and inviting. Echo wasn't sure she'd ever want to leave the bed.

Echo had lost track of time. It had to be late. The night sky was the perfect backdrop to the windows. Mindi had turned on a lamp near the couch that gave off a soft light.

She and Mindi were entwined in the bed, buried beneath the heavy blanket. Echo didn't know what to think about her night with Mindi.

She'd had lovers before, but no one who had worshiped her body the way Mindi had. The woman hadn't even blinked an eye at the stomach rolls or her thick thighs.

Mindi had taken her time and tasted every inch of Echo's body.

Even their animals had risen to the surface. They had nipped each other, leaving little marks on their skin that would be gone soon. Shifters were quick to heal, and little love markings would be completely gone.

Echo's bear still paced, not satisfied that none of the bites had been a claiming one.

Echo observed Mindi who was asleep. She peered down at the sight of Mindi's shoulder, and she, too, was disappointed her mark wasn't there.

The urge to claim this wolf was increasing the longer she was around her.

Her bear sat and licked her lips.

Bite her.

Echo shook her head. She couldn't—wouldn't—force a mating on someone. That would be worse than an arranged mating.

No, she would be patient and wait for Mindi to come around.

Echo was sure Mindi's wolf identified her as a mate. There was no way in the seven hells she didn't.

Glancing back at the windows, she wasn't sure how long they had until morning, but Echo knew she wanted another taste of Mindi.

She didn't know what was going to happen coming morning, but she wanted to take advantage of her time with Mindi.

"What are you thinking about so hard?" Mindi murmured. She closed the small gap between them. She moved lower in the bed and lifted Echo's breast. The woman had suckled them practically all night. She was a boob woman.

Echo groaned when Mindi's lips closed around her nipple. The bud was still sensitive from Mindi's attention, but Echo wasn't going to complain.

Mindi suckled it hard, scraping her fangs against it. A jolt of electricity rippled through Echo's body. Her core clenched, growing moist.

As always, her body was immediately responding to Mindi.

Echo lay on her back and allowed Mindi to have her way with her breasts. Mindi's small hand squeezed her breast while she continued to feast on the other one.

Mindi growled, and Echo whimpered at the sound. She pinched Echo's nipple and tugged on it. The pain was felt so good. Echo's back arched off the bed. She was unable to control her body.

Mindi released Echo's mound and dropped kisses on her sternum. She positioned herself over Echo to allow her to capture the other breast with her lips.

Echo dove her fingers into Mindi's dark hair and held her in place. Mindi took her time bathing this one with her tongue. Echo threw her head back, moans slipping from her. Her thighs were coated with her wetness.

She bit her lip to keep from crying out. The

scent of her and Mindi's arousal filled the air. She licked her lips. She wanted another taste of Mindi.

"Mindi," Echo gasped. She tugged on Mindi's hair to lift her to meet her gaze. "I want my mouth on your pussy."

"You will, in due time." Mindi smirked. She leaned down and pressed a hard kiss to Echo's lips. "Right now, I'm a little busy."

Her amber eyes glowed, and her fangs peeked from underneath her lip. The woman was downright sexy and wore the 'I was just thoroughly fucked' look well. Her eyes grew hooded as she gazed upon Echo's breasts.

"Mindi, I want you to ride my face," Echo announced boldly. She reached out and cupped Mindi's face, bringing it back to hers. She kissed Mindi with everything she had. Her tongue forced its way inside her mouth, stroking Mindi's tongue.

Echo took control. She roved her hands over Mindi's soft body. She had memorized every facet of Mindi's physique. She slotted a hand between Mindi's legs, finding her pussy drenched. She dipped her finger into her core and gathered some of her cream on her fingers.

She brought it up to her lips and licked them clean.

"I want the honey directly from the pot," Echo said.

Mindi's eyes were locked on the sight of Echo's fingers resting on her lips.

"Fuck. Whatever you want." Mindi pushed the covers off them and knelt on the bed.

Echo's heart raced at the sight of her lover's perfect body.

Echo moved the extra pillows from underneath her head and grew excited. Mindi gently threw her leg over Echo's head and straddled her. Echo gripped her hips and guided her down to take a seat.

Echo opened her mouth and immediately suckled Mindi's clit. They groaned simultaneously. Echo slowly suckled the little bundle of nerves. There was no rushing this.

"Oh, Echo," Mindi sighed, rocking her hips.

Echo tightened her grip on Mindi's waist. She was in heaven. She released Mindi's clit and trailed her tongue through the delicious pussy. It was warm, and the tasty juices covered her face. She dipped her tongue into Mindi's core, dragging it out along the entire length of her.

The taste of her lover exploded on her tongue. She took advantage of having Mindi so exposed over her. She made her way back to Mindi's clit and latched on to it.

Mindi cried out, her hips thrusting. She rode Echo's face, taking her pleasure.

She glanced down and held Echo's gaze. Mindi reached down and held Echo's head as if to hold her in place, so her tongue flicked her clit in the same spot.

Mindi shivered, her hand tightening in Echo's hair.

Time appeared to stand still.

Something strong passed through them. Her bear felt Mindi's wolf.

They were destined for each other.

Echo put her complete focus on the little nub in her mouth. She rolled it with her tongue, suckled it until Mindi threw her head back, bellowing her release. Her body shook uncontrollably.

Mindi's cream flooded out of her, and Echo licked it all up. The sweet goodness was now one of her favorite tastes.

Mindi slid her body over Echo. They wrapped their arms around each other. Silence filled the loft.

"Thank you," Echo murmured, brushing Mindi's hair from her sweat-soaked forehead.

Pride filled her that she had caused this look of complete satisfaction on her mate's face.

"You don't have to thank me for that." Mindi chuckled. Her cheeks were flushed; her chest was still rising and falling fast.

Echo hesitated, unsure if she should bring up what was between them. Would now be appropriate?

She was confused.

"I can't get enough of you," Echo said softly. She needed something from Mindi. She didn't want this to just be a passing fancy for her.

They were mates, for goddess sakes.

How could Mindi ignore it?

"Same for me." Mindi's hand skated across her torso and rested on her ample ass, giving it a quick squeeze. She looked at the nightstand clock then faced Echo with a crooked grin. "Now it's my turn."

"Why haven't I seen you since the party?" Rovel demanded.

Echo grimaced and held her phone away from her ear to save her poor eardrum.

"Dad, I've been busy at my bakery. You do remember I own a very success business, right?"

"That doesn't mean you don't call or come by to see your old man," he grumbled.

Echo laughed and sat on her bed. She had just got out of the shower. Work had been busy. They had quite a few custom orders that came in. One for a young bear's sweet sixteen birthday. They had ordered two hundred cupcakes. She and the crew had been hard at work ensuring they would be ready, along with the other orders. By the time she had got home, there was flour coating almost every inch of her.

"I promise I will be over soon."

"You better. We have a lot to talk about this mating. I hear you haven't sat down and spoke with Hyde yet."

And this was the real reason her father had called. Not that she didn't think he didn't miss her, she was sure he did, but the mating was the center of his attention.

"Well, the one day he showed up at the bakery I was on my way out to meet with a client." She might as well continue on with this little white lie. "And don't worry, I'll be having dinner with him tomorrow night."

She couldn't put Hyde off any longer. The bear was very stubborn and persistent.

"Good. Your uncle and I were just talking, and we think our family and Hyde's would be good together."

She rolled her eyes at the statement.

"Again, Dad. I say this to you and to Uncle Trion, you could have at least asked for my opinion. There are plenty of other families we could have contemplated." She couldn't believe she was saying this. She didn't want an arranged mating.

She wanted her mate.

Mindi.

"Oh? Such as who?" he asked.

"Off the top of my head, I don't know, but had you two included me, we could have discussed this more in detail," she huffed.

"Well, it's too late for that. You need to mate to a bear. We have to do our part to ensure our clan remains strong."

"Dad, why a bear? What if that was the problem? Maybe our mates aren't bears."

"Mating with something other than a bear? You know the rules. How will we guarantee any children from those unions will result in bear cubs?"

There it was again. The future. The elders of

the clan were so set on ensuring bear cubs were produced that they didn't even care if anyone would be happy in their pairings.

"Dad, can we at least consider that maybe my mate is not a bear?"

"Your mate is a bear." Her father's voice grew firm.

Echo knew that meant he was done with the discussion.

"Now, I don't want to hear any other talk about this. You will mate with Hyde. He's a fine young man, strong, and will be a good provider. He's a little rough around the edges, but I'm sure you can smooth him out to your liking."

"Dad," she groaned. She coasted a hand over her face. Frustration filled her. Why did her clan have to believe in such craziness? Maybe that was the problem. They weren't even given the chance to find love elsewhere. Just because someone was a bear, didn't mean they were the best choice for her. "I love you, Dad."

Now was not the time to get in an argument with him. What she had to focus on was getting Mindi to admit they were mates. She had been thinking long and hard about it. If she could get Mindi to see what was between them, and that they could have all the good things in life together, then she could get the agreement between her and Hyde's family voided.

Who would argue against fate?

Certainly, her clan would understand that fate had paired her with a wolf, not a bear.

Fate had to count for something. Echo was willing to go before her father, her uncle, hell, every elder in her clan to prove it.

She only had to get the nerve to do it.

"I love you, too, baby girl. No more talk about finding a mate. Everything is handled." He sighed. "When are you coming over to cook for your old man?"

She laughed at his abrupt change in the conversation. He had made her promise that when she moved out on her own that she would still come over and cook for him. She was extremely close with her father and brothers.

"Why don't we find a day when all of us can get together, and I'll cook us a feast."

"I'll call Vick and Cole and see when they are free. It would be good to have all of my children home. It's just not the same without you three hollering and screaming at each other."

"Too quiet?" She smirked. She pushed off the

bed and dried off with her towel. She snagged her nightshirt and threw it on.

When they were kids, her father would roar, shouting that all he wanted was peace and quiet. Her brothers were always getting into some kind of trouble and would rope Echo in on the shenanigans, too.

"Yes, it is. Now, once I get you three mated off, hopefully that will mean grandbabies." Her father's voice grew gruff.

Her heart softened at the thought of her father being lonely.

Maybe what he needed was a companion.

A mate.

Now she was going to have to call her brothers and bring them in on this. They couldn't be the only ones being made to mate.

She loved her mother dearly, and she had been gone since Echo was young, but her father shouldn't have to live out the rest of his life lonely.

If he found someone who he could spend time with then maybe he would leave her, and her brothers' lives, alone.

"Let's take this one step at a time, Dad." She yawned and combed her hands through her wet hair. She exited her room and headed toward the living room.

"I hear you yawning. You shouldn't be working so hard. Go get some rest, baby."

"Okay, Dad. I'll call you later."

They disconnected their call with her promising to swing by. She tossed her phone on the couch and went over to the large window. The moon was high. It wasn't a full one, about a half. She glanced at it and wondered where Mindi was.

Was she looking up at the moon, too?

Echo left her house and sat on the front steps. She breathed in the scent of nature. Her ears picked up the sounds of wild animals out in the woods.

Her bear, sensing the outdoors, growled.

She wanted out.

"Fine." Echo sighed. She stood and removed her clothes and put them in a neat pile. She turned and allowed the change to come.

Her dark fur burst forward, while her bones contorted and lengthened. She fell to the ground, kneeling until she completely shifted into her beast.

Her bear gave a satisfied groan, then trotted off into the woods.

CHAPTER SEVEN

M indi walked into the restaurant for a consult with potential clients. She had been invited to dinner by Jackal and Leslie, a newly mated couple who wanted to hire Mindi for their couple's shoot. Mindi had known Jackal, a member of her pack, for a long time and was honored he'd wanted to include her in their celebrating their mating. He had played football with her brother in high school and had reached out to Dirk for her services.

Now Jackal was another one of the wolves who had found his mate and fallen head over heels in love with his human. Mindi smiled walking through the establishment. They were to convene at the bar to discuss details of what they were looking for.

Mindi arrived at the bar a few minutes earlier than their scheduled meeting.

It was a busy night. Servers rushed around attending to their tables.

"Can I get you something?" The barkeep came to stand in front of her.

"I'm waiting on some friends," Mindi announced.

"All right, I'll be back to check on you." He tossed her a wink and moved on to another newcomer who had pulled up to the counter.

Mindi took a seat and hefted her messenger bag on her shoulder. She didn't have long to wait before Jackal and Leslie arrived. He was a tall wolf standing just above six feet, with long dark hair, broad shoulders, and mischievous eyes. No wonder his parents named him Jackal. Leslie was the complete opposite, around the same height as Mindi, with warm brown skin, honey-brown eyes, and a welcoming smile.

"Mindi, how the hell are you?" Jackal slapped her on her back.

"I'm doing well, thanks." Mindi swiveled

around in her chair to face them. She turned her attention to Leslie. "And this must be Leslie."

"It is." Jackal grinned brightly, making the introductions.

Mindi and Leslie shook hands. It was the first time the two women had met. Ever since Leslie had moved to Howling Valley, Jackal had been rarely seen. From what Mindi had heard from her brother, the wolf had to learn to court his human mate to get her to trust him.

From the looks of the woman's smile, Jackal had succeeded.

"My brother tells me you would like a couple photo shoot?" Mindi's eyebrows rose. She didn't think Jackal was the type of wolf who was sentimental enough to want to capture his love for his mate on film.

"It was my idea." Leslie raised her hand and giggled.

"That makes more sense." Mindi snickered.

"Hey." Jackal elbowed Mindi. "I'm the one who told her about you."

"I've been wanting to do photos, but then a certain persistent wolf captured my eye and wouldn't leave me alone until I became his mate." Leslie turned to her mate with big love-filled eyes.

"Like I could stay away from you," Jackal murmured, kissing the top of her head.

A slight pain crossed through Mindi's chest. Mating. This was what it looked like. True love, happiness, and fulfilling each other's needs.

Her wolf prowled inside her, giving a hard snort.

Echo's face appeared in her mind.

Mindi's wolf whined, scratching at her stomach.

Mindi bit back a sigh and tried to get her wolf to sit down. They couldn't think of mating at the moment. Echo was in contracts with another, and who was Mindi to go and break up the archaic tradition?

Her true mate, her wolf snapped.

"I brought my portfolio for you to browse through so I can get a sense of what exactly you are looking for." Mindi pulled her leather binder from her bag and sat it on the counter.

"I've been all over your website, so I know you do amazing work," Leslie gushed.

"Hey, I see your friends arrived. Can I get you anything to drink?" the bartender returned, interrupting. He quickly took their orders before disappearing again.

"We have plenty of options," Mindi began, opening the book.

"I'll be right back. I need to run to the restroom." Jackal dropped a kiss on Leslie's shoulder and ambled away.

Mindi couldn't help but notice how Jackal had continuously touched Leslie in some way. He was a doting male, protecting his mate and showing affection. Mindi swallowed hard.

Deep down, she wanted that connection—

Mate.

Her wolf was going to drive her crazy. She had to let Echo go. She was going to be mated to another.

Leslie watched Jackal enter the men's room then turned back to Mindi with a mischievous glint in her eyes.

"I hear you do boudoir shoots," Leslie stated.

"I do." Mindi chuckled.

The barkeep brought their drinks and dropped them off. Mindi gave him a nod and picked up her glass. She took a sip, spinning back to Leslie.

"Good. I would love to do spicy photos to give them to Jack for his birthday."

"We can come up with something without him

knowing." Mindi nodded. Plenty of women came to her wanting to do these private shoots.

"Great." Leslie danced in her chair and reached for her drink.

Mindi pushed her portfolio to Leslie who took the seat next to her. They began discussing what Leslie's vision was.

"These are just so beautiful. You've captured all of the emotion and love in their eyes."

Mindi sat back, pride filling her. She worked hard to make sure emotions were expressed in all of her works. The desire to have people connect with her photos was strong. It was the artist in her, wanting to share beauty with the world.

They continued going through the book with Mindi sharing stories of the people who had allowed her to capture special moments.

"All right, ladies. Why don't we get a table?" Jackal returned to them. He scooped up his drink and took a hefty sip of it. "My treat."

"You don't have to—"

"Yes, we do." Leslie slid from her chair. She hefted up the book and her glass. "Come. Let's have dinner."

Apparently, Jackal had secured a table while Mindi and Leslie had been engrossed in the photos.

"Well, since you asked so nicely," Mindi joked. She picked up her glass and handed some bills to the barkeeper to pay for their drinks.

"What are you doing?" Jackal laughed. "Your money is no good here."

"I'll pay for the drinks, and you get the dinner tab." Mindi grinned. Who was she to try to keep a man in love from spoiling his woman and their photographer?

"Deal." Jackal slapped her on the back and guided her and Leslie through the restaurant.

Mindi's wolf paced, unsettled for some reason. Mindi tried to shake it off. She took another sip of her drink and adjusted the strap of her bag on her shoulder.

Loud laughter filled the air. Mindi's gaze scanned the area and landed on Echo sitting at a table with Hyde.

Their eyes connected.

Mindi's breath escaped her as she'd received a blow to the stomach.

Her wolf growled, not liking how close the asshole was sitting next to Echo.

Mindi gave a curt nod to Echo. The memory of their night together flooded her.

She arrived at the table with Jackal and Leslie.

Jackal, the doting wolf, assisted his mate into her chair.

"Will you excuse me for a moment?" Mindi sat her glass down on the table and her bag on her chair. "I see someone I know and want to say hi."

"But of course. We'll be waiting on you." Jackal took a seat next to Leslie.

Mindi made her way to Echo's table.

"Good evening," Mindi said, stopping in front of their table.

Echo's eyes widened as she stared at her.

"Ah, Mindi, isn't it? You're Mick's daughter," Hyde announced. He picked up his glass mug and tipped it to her.

"Yes, I am. I'm here with clients and wanted to stop and say hello." Mindi greedily took in Echo who was dressed in a soft wraparound dress that accented her full figure. Mindi's wolf stood at the scent of their mate slowly filtering through the air toward her. Mindi inhaled the aroma and bit back a growl.

"That was quite nice of you. Thank you for swinging by our engagement party the other night. It was good to see the support of the wolves." Hyde sat back and put an arm around Echo who flinched. "We really appreciate it."

"Yes. Congratulations on your upcoming mating." Mindi put her hands in her pockets to keep from forming fists. Suddenly she had the urge to punch Hyde straight in the face. She didn't think it would go over well for her to beat the bear to a pulp in public.

"I'm a lucky bastard for being matched with a woman like Echo." He squeezed Echo's shoulders and boasted a boisterous laugh.

Mindi licked her lips, which were suddenly extremely dry. She stared at Echo, remembering the taste of her on her tongue.

"Yes, you are one lucky man." Mindi tried not to snarl that last remark. It was becoming harder to walk away from Echo.

She didn't belong to Hyde.

It didn't matter there was a contract and their relationship was arranged.

She belonged to Mindi.

"I don't want to hold you two up. Have a wonderful dinner." Mindi nodded to Hyde then Echo. She spun around on her heels and ambled back over to Jackal and Leslie. As much as she wanted, she couldn't snatch Echo from Hyde's grasp and drag her away from him.

Her wolf howled, not understanding why they weren't staying with Echo.

"There she is," Jackal announced.

"Sorry about that." Mindi slid into her seat across from the couple. "Anything you recommend?"

She reached for the menu and flipped it open. She'd only ever eaten here a few times. This restaurant was one of the fancier ones in town.

"They have a great steak selection." Leslie motioned to the page she was looking at.

Mindi nodded and turned her menu to that page. A good steak did sound good. She wasn't sure how she was going to get through dinner without focusing on Echo. The scent of her still consumed Mindi.

She was going to have to come to the ultimate decision.

Would she go ahead and claim her mate, or let Hyde?

The force of her wolf slamming into her chest let her know the answer.

But how was she going to get Echo from the large bear?

CHAPTER EIGHT

Echo's heart was pounding a mile a minute. She couldn't believe Mindi was there in the flesh. The moment Echo's eyes connected with Mindi's, she couldn't think of anything else. Hyde had been blabbing about something that no longer held her attention. She didn't give a damn about what he had to say.

Her wolf was walking toward her.

Mindi was the epitome of sexy businesswoman. She was dressed in a white button-down shirt, slacks, and killer heels. Her thick hair had been left down, and the sexiest part of her outfit was her damn suspenders.

Who would have thought that would have made an outfit?

Just taking in Mindi while she pretended to care what Hyde was saying had her bear ready to pounce. It took everything Echo had not to shift.

Echo knew the true reasons Mindi had come to their table.

One, to let Echo know she was in the building, and two, to remind Echo of everything they had done to and with each other while she was with her betrothed.

They had to be the only reasons she had stopped by.

Echo was so confused by the wolf. One moment she acted as if she didn't feel the pull to mate, then she came over to their table with the silent reminder of what they had between them.

Hyde didn't catch on to any of it, but it was plain as day for Echo.

Echo didn't miss the deepening of Mindi's eyes at Hyde mentioning how lucky he was to have her. Nor did she miss the clenching of Mindi's hands into fists.

The wolf could try to deny it all she wanted, but

the truth was, fate wanted them to be together.

Echo prayed her wolf came around.

She couldn't imagine having to spend a lifetime with Hyde.

I don't want to hold you two up. Have a wonderful dinner.

And then Mindi was gone. She'd only stopped by for a brief moment.

Echo sighed and watched Mindi walk back to her table where a couple sat engrossed in a book.

Echo wished she could have invited Mindi to stay with them. Having her here would have been a buffer between her and Hyde, but it wouldn't have been right.

Her bear wanted Mindi and was determined to go to her every chance she got.

"Somebody's bear is awfully close," Hyde murmured. His eyes darkened, and a rumble vibrated from his chest. He leaned over and inhaled her scent. A smirk appeared on his face.

Oh, goodness.

He was apparently thinking her bear was close to the surface because of him. Echo reached for her drink and took a healthy sip, not wanting to bruise his ego with the knowledge that he didn't do anything for her.

"Soon, we will complete our mating." He patted her on her hand and dove back into his food.

Echo grimaced and returned to her plate. At least that was appealing. Being in an arranged mating was similar to a human's wedding ceremony and celebration. They would exchange vows in front of their clan, then they would go off to claim each other. The claiming bite wouldn't be that of a true mate, but they would carry the marking of each other. She would belong to Hyde, and he would be hers. Disgust filled her at the thought of him hovering above her and then sinking his fangs into her.

She needed to figure something out fast.

Her clan loved to celebrate, so she was sure they were already planning a huge party. Her father and Hyde's were proud of the match, and she assumed bears from all over would be invited to attend.

She groaned internally. She had to find a way out of this. If she waited until it was too late, then she'd find herself hitched to Hyde in front of their entire clan and family.

"Anyway, as I was saying before that wolf showed up, we can live in my cabin. It's much bigger than yours," Hyde continued.

Echo determined the bear must love hearing

himself talk. Yes, they were here to discuss their upcoming mating, but could they at least eat in peace? He just kept blabbering on.

Echo stole a glance over at Mindi's table. The woman was beautiful, and the female said something that made her smile.

Jealousy filled Echo.

She wanted to be at dinner with Mindi, making her smile and then leaving to go back to either of their places.

Echo would love to invite Mindi to her place. Her cabin in the woods was perfect for the two of them. She imagined them snuggled up on her couch on the back porch. She had just purchased new outdoor furniture, and the couch was oversized, and she wasn't sure why she'd bought it.

Now she knew.

It was made for two.

With a sigh, Echo tore her gaze from Mindi. She took a sip of her tea and turned back to Hyde who was still talking.

Maybe she should have had an alcoholic drink. It would have made this dinner a little more interesting.

"Our children would hold high positions in the clan."

Echo blinked. What did he just say?

"Excuse me?" Echo said.

"Our cubs." Hyde grinned and reached for his napkin. He wiped his hands on it and sat back in his chair. "Our sons could be lead enforcers. I'm sure they will be big and strong. With my size and yours, our boys will be great grizzlies who will be protecting our clan."

"Um, yeah, I guess." An enforcer was a high-ranking position amongst the clan. It would be an honor to have her child join the ranking of some of the great enforcers. Without a doubt, her uncle would promote his great-nephews or niece to that position if they were worthy.

"Look, I'm not that bad, Echo. I'm sure you will come around to this mating." He leaned over and took her hand in his.

He kissed the back of it, and Echo held back a grimace.

"It was just all so sudden." She sighed. Echo didn't want to insult him to his face and tell him he wouldn't have been any of her choices as a mate had she known she was being forced into an arrangement.

"We'll both get something out of this mating.

No one else may have wanted you, but I see the bigger picture."

"What?" She snatched her hand back from him. "What do you mean no one wanted me?"

"I didn't mean it that way," he sputtered. He tried to backtrack, but it was too late. "I just meant some men weren't too keen on signing up for an arranged mating—"

"I think you've said enough." Echo was embarrassed and pissed. And here she was trying to spare his feelings.

Her bear, on the other hand, wanted to burst free and break things.

No one wanted her.

How about no one was worthy of her.

"Don't get upset, Echo." Hyde shrugged. "It's nothing to worry about it."

"How can I not worry about it? There's nothing wrong with me, and you just drop a bomb on me that I was unwanted?" She bit out the last of her words through clenched teeth.

"Like I said, don't worry about it. You've got me." He grinned and apparently wasn't understanding why she was upset. He finished off his beer and slammed the mug down. "And you're mine."

"Hyde, you hated me when we were kids. I find it funny that you accepted the match." Echo glared at him, not holding anything back. She was normally a pushover, but if he was going to be her mate, then he was going to have to know the real Echo. "Why?"

His grin disappeared, and he returned her stare.

"Because I see the bigger picture. You are my key to ensure my future generation is secured in this clan."

"Is that so?"

Her gaze wandered around, scanning the restaurant. Echo knew someone who at least appreciated her and was meant for her.

She just had to convince the stubborn wolf they needed to take the leap of faith.

Tired, Mindi let herself into her building. She went upstairs and immediately kicked off her heels. She beelined it to her stash of spirits and poured herself a stiff drink. She then unbuttoned her shirt and removed her bra.

"That's better," she breathed. She walked over

to her closet and tossed the contraption in her laundry basket.

Leaving her shirt unbuttoned, she figured she wouldn't change until it was time for bed. At the moment she wanted to go finish developing the photos she'd been working on.

She padded down the stairs to her darkroom on the lower level. When she'd first discovered the building was set to be demolished, Mindi had quickly put a bid in on it. Howling Valley had designated it to be torn down and rezoned. It was at the edge of town and was perfect.

When she'd submitted her proposal to turn it into a photography studio and a loft, the council had approved it immediately.

Before, Mindi had been working out of her parents' basement. She had scraped and saved money until she was ready to start looking for somewhere to live.

The idea to have a historic building renovated into a living and working space knocked two birds out with one stone.

Her father had given her the extra money she had needed for the construction cost. Her parents were big supporters of her dream to become a photographer.

Adele Martin had purchased Mindi's first camera when she was five years old. She had taken notice that her youngest daughter loved taking pictures every time she stole Adele's. The second Mindi had her brand-new camera, she was off in the woods getting lost trying to take the best pictures a five-year-old could muster.

Anything she could capture on film, she did. Birds, bees, deer, and even the occasional shifter walking along in the woods.

Mindi just loved being behind the camera.

She sold her first picture to the local library when she was only six years old. Her bright mind had fallen in love with the idea of making money off of her artwork. She began going around town, offering her photos for sale.

It was that first transaction which gave Mindi the confidence to pursue her dream.

Photography was her true passion.

Her wolf snorted.

Mate.

"Okay, I'm going to figure that out," she muttered. She arrived in the lower-level room. She flipped on the switch, bathing the room in a low red light.

Her darkroom was her sanctuary. It was here

where she developed her masterpieces. She loved watching the photos come to life in her hand.

Mindi took another sip of her drink then settled the glass on the table near her station. The room was filled with everything she needed. She had placed a small couch in the corner. There were plenty of days where she tired and crashed on her couch while working.

Getting to work, she began to develop photos she had taken the other day. As with all parts of her job, she became lost in her work and the time.

As much as she wanted to push Echo from her mind, her wolf wasn't going to allow it to happen, and neither was her heart.

She glanced down at the post-orgasmic snapshots of Echo. The woman was gorgeous. Every part of her body tasted delightful. If Mindi paused and concentrated, she could almost taste her.

Echo wasn't a passing fancy like all of the other women in her life before Mindi had met the bear shifter.

She was definitely a good fuck, but that wasn't all she was.

Who was she kidding?

There was no way she could ignore what was between them.

Mindi knew it deep down in her heart.

She was going to have to follow her wolf's lead.

Her beast sat up and wagged her bushy tail. It was rare Mindi gave her animal the reins to lead.

Mindi grinned and carried the photo over to the drying line and hung it up.

Her phone beeped, alerting her of someone ringing the bell to the side door. It was the private entrance to her building instead of using the storefront.

Curious, Mindi wondered who would be stopping by this late. Usually, any of her prior lovers knew to call ahead before showing up.

She marched over to the table and grabbed her phone. She swiped her finger across the glass screen and pulled up the security camera.

Mindi's heart raced at the sight of the figure standing by the door.

Echo.

Mindi knocked back the rest of her drink and sat the glass back down. The amber liquid burned on its way down. She took her time walking up the stairs to the door. She opened it and leaned against the doorjamb.

Echo stood with her wide eyes and a ghost of a smile on her plump lips. Her dark hair pooled around her shoulders. Her hands held her purse strap in a death grip.

"May I come in?" Echo asked, her voice low and husky.

They stared at each other for another moment. Mindi jerked her head in a nod and waved her in.

"I'm so sorry for coming by so late." Echo brushed past Mindi.

The scent of her perfume and natural aroma surrounded Mindi. She breathed it in and tried to play it cool. Her wolf's initial reaction was to drag Echo upstairs, but she held back. Her animal paced back and forth, sensing Echo's presence.

"It's okay. I was down in the darkroom working." Mindi shut the door and locked it. She waved for Echo to follow her. "Come. I want to show you something."

Mindi jogged down the stairs with Echo following behind her.

"Why are you working so late?" Echo asked.

"Can't sleep, but I really wanted to see how these turned out." Mindi motioned to the drying area.

Echo gasped, walking around the photos in awe as if she didn't realize how beautiful she was.

Mindi's wolf rammed her.

Claim her.

Mindi pushed her animal back. It was getting harder to fight her. She couldn't just jump Echo and take her with force.

Mindi swallowed, watching Echo's eyes light up as she paused at each photo. Echo arrived at a new row and froze in place.

"Oh my. These are breathtaking. I don't even know what to say." Echo glanced over at her.

Mindi ambled over to her to see which ones she was looking at. Mindi smirked. She knew Echo hadn't known she'd put the camera on auto-shoot.

Echo's attention was captivated by the ones of them together. "These with the two of us are so…I don't know what to say, but I love them. Can I have copies?"

"Of course." Mindi leaned against the counter and watched her continue on. The ones of them together making love were Mindi's favorite. She'd never participated in a photo shoot with another before. It just came to her at the last moment, and the vision she had in that brief second had paid off. The photos were sensual and a thing of beauty. "Which ones do you want?"

"All of them."

CHAPTER NINE

W ho the hell was this siren? Sex symbol. A luscious woman with sex appeal.

Echo had a hard time believing it was herself on the photos. Mindi definitely knew what she was doing when it came to the camera.

Even the ones of her and Mindi having sex were astounding.

The way the camera caught them made it almost poetic or a tasteful piece of artwork of lovers in the throes of passion.

Echo glanced over at Mindi who was braced against the counter. Echo's throat tightened at the sight of the wolf. She was the epitome of sexiness. The button-down shirt was open enough to give a peek at her abdomen and the swell of her breasts. Her slacks were perfectly tailored to her, and her suspenders hung down by her sides. Her tiny toes peeked out front underneath the hem of her pants.

Mindi's amber-eyed gaze tracked Echo's movements like a hunter stalking her prey.

Echo turned back to the next photo and inhaled sharply. The camera somehow captured her in the midst of her orgasm with Mindi's face buried between her thighs.

She remembered that moment.

Her stomach muscles clenched. She flicked her gaze over to Mindi who was still watching her.

Echo's bear stood on her hind legs and rumbled a growl.

Claim her.

Echo took a step back from the pictures and slowly ambled over to Mindi.

"You are amazing," Echo breathed. She stopped within a hairsbreadth of Mindi. Her gaze dropped down to Mindi's pink lips, then moved down to the column of her neck. Echo's gums burned from her fangs threatening to burst forth. Unable to resist touching Mindi, Echo rested a finger on her sternum. "I can't stop thinking about you."

She trailed her finger over the smooth expanse of skin and ended at her belly button.

"Same here." Mindi's husky voice greeted her ears.

Echo glanced up and met Mindi's heated stare.

She brushed aside the open shirt with her finger to reveal one of Mindi's perfect breasts. The beaded nipples were tempting. Echo remembered how sweet they were. She boldly reached up and pushed Mindi's shirt off onto the floor.

Now that the offending item was gone, Echo reached up and cupped both of the perfect mounds. Mindi's silky skin fueled the desire for her inside Echo. It raged throughout her body like a wildfire.

Mindi's soft moan broke the silence in the air. Echo massaged her, pinching her nipples between her thumb and forefinger. Mindi's head fell back, her hands gripping the counter behind her.

Echo leaned forward and kissed the hollow of Mindi's neck. She breathed in her womanly scent, and her bear roared.

Their mate was near, and she was growing aroused.

The faint scent of Mindi's sweetness was filling the room.

Echo trailed hot kisses down Mindi's neck and stepped closer to her, leaving no room between them.

She slid her hands over Mindi's body, exploring the toned muscles of her stomach and resting on her waist.

Echo softly sank her teeth into the meat of Mindi's shoulder in a love bite. It wasn't the bite she wanted to do. Her bear snarled, not pleased it wasn't the mating bite.

Soon, she whispered to her bear. Her animal appeared to calm at the promise. This woman before her was hers. At the moment, she wouldn't think of her clan's rules nor the upcoming mating with Hyde.

All Echo wanted to do was lose herself in Mindi.

She moved her lips to Mindi's throat. She finally arrived at Mindi's lips and captured them in a hard, brutal kiss.

Echo moaned, Mindi's tongue stroking hers, inviting her farther inside her mouth. The kiss turned frantic.

Mindi's fingers threaded their way into Echo's

hair and held her close as their kiss deepened. Echo's body was on fire. She needed a release that only Mindi could give her.

Mindi broke their kiss and rested her forehead on Echo's.

"Why don't we take this upstairs?"

Echo nodded and stepped back away from Mindi. She brushed past her and cut the lights out. Mindi took Echo's hand and stalked toward the stairs, pulling Echo along.

They arrived at Mindi's private living area. The wolf tugged Echo over to her sleeping area. Mindi turned to her when they made it to her bed. The faced each other, ripping their clothes off.

Echo had never had this type of urgency before. The need to put her mouth all over Mindi's body consumed her.

They fell onto the bed in a tangle of limbs. Mindi's lips were everywhere. She took Echo's mouth in a deep, soul-searing kiss. She rolled Echo over onto her back and settled on top of her.

Their breasts were pushed against each other. Echo moaned, loving the sensation of Mindi's nipples brushing hers. Their bodies molded together as they writhed in rhythm with each other.

Mindi trailed hot kisses over Echo's neck and

shoulder. She continued on down to Echo's breasts. Her lips enclosed around Echo's nipple.

A groan escaped Echo. Her hands dove into Mindi's hair, holding her captive.

"Yes," Echo hissed.

Mindi scraped her fangs along the taut bud, eliciting a cry from her.

"Hold on." Mindi's crooked grin spread across her face. She winked at Echo and rolled over on the mattress and opened her nightstand drawer.

Echo turned on her side and eyed Mindi's perfect form. Her ass was nice and round. Echo licked her lips, wanting to taste every inch of the wolf.

"What are you doing?" Echo giggled.

"Let's have some fun." Mindi faced Echo with a toy in her hand.

Echo stared at it, taking in the wide cock shape. The silicone cock was dark blue in color, curved and lined with ridges. There was a looped handle that Echo was sure allowed the person using it to control it better.

"Oh boy." She inhaled sharply. The devilish glint in Mindi's eye told her that she was in for long night of pleasure.

"You trust that I'll only give you pleasure,

right?" Mindi asked as if reading Echo's mind. She scooted back next to Echo and rested a hand on her thigh.

She didn't hesitate in her answer. "Yes."

"Good." Mindi pressed a kiss on Echo's nipple, her hand skating along her thigh to her core. She dipped her fingers into Echo's slick folds. She toyed with her clit while laving Echo's nipple with her tongue. "Just lie back and relax. Let me take care of you."

Echo moaned, trying to rest against the pillows. Mindi's touch always sent a bolt of lightning through her. How could she not move?

Echo closed her eyes and put her trust in Mindi's capable hands.

Mindi continued working Echo's nipple with her tongue. Her fingers slid through her folds, dipping inside Echo's hot core. Echo could feel the proof of her desire coating her thighs.

"Always so wet for me," Mindi murmured, her lips brushing Echo's nipple. Her chest rumbled with her wolf's growl. "My Echo."

Her breath caught in her throat. Mindi rested the tip of the toy on her bundle of nerves. Soon the vibrator was on the move. Mindi guided it through her folds, coating it with her juices.

Echo's muscles tensed in anticipation.

The tip of the silicone cock paused at her entrance.

Mindi teased her nipple, drawing a moan from Echo. At that moment, Mindi slowly introduced the cock into Echo.

A moan slipped from her lips again. Her body quivered from the thick invasion.

The ridges.

Its wide girth stretched Echo, stealing the air from her. She tried to breathe but was unable to drag in air. Mindi pushed it in until it couldn't go any farther.

"Oh, goddess above." The words tumbled from Echo's lips.

Mindi worked it in and out of her. She twisted it around, extracting a cry from Echo once it hit her spot.

Echo's hips moved in rhythm with Mindi. Her claws burst forth, shredding the sheets underneath her as she held on. The poor mattress would suffer, but the pleasure was too good to resist.

The bed shifted while Mindi moved to position herself between Echo's legs. She pushed Echo's leg into the air, sending the toy deeper.

"Someone likes my new toy." Mindi chuckled.

"Yes." Echo gave a throaty groan.

Then the vibration began.

Echo was beside herself. She bucked and moaned, grinding her pussy against the toy. She took all of the pleasure her mate was bestowing upon her.

Mindi's other hand glided down and strummed Echo's clit while quickening the thrusts of the cock.

It was too much.

Whimpering, she threw her head back. She was so close to losing control and allowing her orgasm to take her.

The cock arched and hit her G-spot, and Echo's body detonated. Her body went rigid, and a scream erupted from her lips. The sound of the mattress ripping was a distant thought. Echo trembled, the waves of her climax washing through her.

She fell back against the bed, her breaths coming hard and fast. She opened her eyes at the sensation of the cock being withdrawn from her.

Mindi tossed the long blue cock to the side and pressed Echo's legs back, opening them wider.

"Hmm...now my turn." Mindi leaned down and swiped Echo's pussy with her tongue.

Echo's eyes rolled into the back of her head.

She held on to the torn mattress, while Mindi licked and lapped up all of her release.

The second her lover latched on to her clit, she tensed, sensing another orgasm was on the horizon.

There was nothing she wanted more than to allow her mate to have her way with her body.

Echo lay back and opened herself to Mindi.

Her body truly belonged to this woman, and the sight of Mindi enjoying her pussy would be forever embedded into her mind.

Echo withdrew her claws and reached down and brushed Echo's hair from her face. Mindi's eyes opened, and she was met with an intense amber gaze.

"Take all of me," Echo whispered. "Tonight, I'm yours."

Mindi swiped her pussy one last time. She pushed up on the bed and climbed over Echo, her body moving like the predator she was. Her amber eyes locked with Echo's. The proof of her release coated Mindi's lips and chin.

Both of their animals made their presence known, low growls filing the silence in the room.

Mindi bent down and took Echo's lips in a deep, passionate kiss. Mindi's soft lips moved on Echo's in a possessive kiss. Echo whimpered and wrapped her arms around Mindi. The faint hint of her own pussy greeted her, but she didn't care.

Echo gasped when Mindi suddenly broke the kiss. She pressed Echo's legs open and arranged hers to allow her to settle down on top of her where their swollen clits brushed each other.

Echo stared up into Mindi's beautiful eyes, becoming lost in them.

"You are mine," Mindi growled. She thrust forward, sliding her nub against Echo's. "Tonight, you belong to me."

"Yes."

Echo pulled Mindi's face down to her. Tonight, they would take each other. Damn anything else. Echo wouldn't worry about anything until morning.

Tonight, she was turning all of herself over to Mindi.

CHAPTER TEN

Echo shifted in the bed onto her side. The blanket fell away, revealing her shoulder. Mindi leaned back against her pillow and eyed the newly bare skin. She licked her lips, tempted to lick and kiss Echo's shoulder.

If she pressed one kiss there, it would be hard to keep from dropping more all over the sexy bear shifter's body.

Echo looked so peaceful in her sleep. Her dark eyelashes rested on her cheeks, while her lips, still swollen from Mindi's kisses, were slightly parted.

The temptation to taste those lips again was strong.

Instead, Mindi reached over and opened her nightstand drawer and took out one of her small handheld cameras.

A woman this beautiful deserved to be captured.

The soft sunrays filtering in through the windows provided soft, natural light. It was the perfect setting without her even having to try to provide one.

Echo's hair was spread out on the white pillows and was a direct contrast. Her smooth tanned skin was creamy, and Mindi knew from experience it was sweet.

Mindi removed the lens cover and flipped the camera on. She peered through the viewfinder and aimed the camera at Echo. She pressed the shutter button, snapping a few pictures.

Mindi paused when Echo moved, stretching her legs out. She rolled slightly on her back. The blanket was dangerously close to falling away from her.

Mindi grinned and pulled the cover off Echo. Her large breasts were now revealed; her dark nipples grew into taut little buds. Mindi zoomed in on Echo's mounds, capturing the beauties in the natural light.

Echo's body was flawless and should be photographed and hung somewhere for all to appreciate.

Mindi shifted on the bed, getting up onto her knees. She wanted to take advantage of the natural look of a woman well-loved.

Echo had Mindi's love marks all over her body. Something resonated inside Mindi as she gazed upon the markings.

Mate her.

Her wolf must have woken up on the wrong side of the bed.

Her animal apparently wasn't happy that none of the hickeys she'd left on Echo were a true claiming bite.

Mindi focused on the swell of Echo's hip when her lover rolled onto her side. She opened an eye, staring at Mindi.

"Oh, come on. It's too early for pictures." Echo groaned. She covered her face with her hand.

It didn't keep Mindi from taking her photos.

"You're beautiful first thing in the morning. I want to capture you waking up," Mindi murmured.

"But I'm naked." Echo tried to hide underneath the blanket.

"Your body should never be covered," Mindi said.

They played tug of war for a moment. Mindi won, dragging the blankets completely off the bed. Their laughter filled the air. Mindi loved the sound of Echo's laugher.

She smiled and gently ran a hand up Echo's calf. "How are you a shifter and shy about your body?"

It just didn't make sense. Their clothes never survived the change. Bears weren't too different than wolves. They were used to being naked around other people. It was normal before and after pack runs.

Echo sighed, then brushed her hair from her face.

"All my life I've been teased about my size. I'm not like most bear shifters. Sure, our women are normally tall, thick, and toned. Me, I'm short and curvy. There's not a defined muscle in my body."

"Whoever teased you about this body is a complete idiot." Mindi aimed the camera at Echo, capturing her emotions on film. Her heart hurt that her mate had to deal with shallow people.

"Most of my clan and even my betrothed made me feel as if I wasn't beautiful when I was growing up."

"Are you shitting me?" Mindi paused and glanced at Echo. By this time, she had stood from the bed and walked around it while she photographed all angles of Echo.

If Hyde wasn't already at the top of her shit list, he was now.

"And he wants to mate with you?" Mindi snarled. Unbelievable. What did her family have to offer to get him to agree to an arranged mating?

"It's an arrangement." Echo shrugged. "It's what's best for our families."

"Well, I hope you don't believe any of those assholes. Echo, you are the most beautiful woman I've ever had the pleasure to know."

Echo's cheeks warmed, a smile appearing on her face. Mindi snapped another picture without even looking through the viewfinder.

"Thank you." A strange look passed over Echo's face.

"Arch your back," Mindi insisted. She brought the camera back up so she could focus on Echo.

Echo bit her lip, a sexy move that Mindi loved. Mindi snapped another picture.

"Now push your boobs together and show them off."

Echo giggled, doing what was asked of her.

"And drop your legs open and show me that pretty pussy."

A moan slipped from Echo. Her smile slowly faded as she spread her legs.

Mindi didn't hesitate on zooming in to capture the sight of Echo's delicious cunt. Her labia were rosy pink, and her clit peeked out from between them.

"Atta girl," Mindi murmured. She crawled back into the bed next to Echo. She pulled up the photos on the display so Echo could review them. "This is what I see when I look at you."

Echo's eyes widened. She took the camera and hit the button to move to the next photo.

Mindi ghosted her hand over Echo's stomach. The urge to claim this woman and put them both out of their misery was strong.

Her gums burned as her fangs descended.

"I shouldn't want you as much as I do," Mindi whispered. She smoothed her hand down Echo's body and dove between her legs. She leaned over and nipped Echo's shoulder. She parted Echo's labia and pushed two of her fingers inside the warm, welcoming channel. It was slick with her juices. "This is just too good to pass up."

"But, Mindi—"

"Look at the pictures I just took," Mindi cut Echo off. She needed Echo to truly believe how beautiful and desirable she was. Echo only half believed she was beautiful. Mindi wanted Echo to forget everything that was ever said to her in the past.

"Well, what about this?" Echo rested a hand on her belly.

"What about it?" Mindi leaned over and kissed it. There was nothing wrong with having a little extra in the middle.

"My fupa?" Echo's hand moved down to her mons. A moan slipped from her lips when Mindi thrust her fingers inside her, hard.

"It houses the sweetest pussy I've ever tasted." Mindi scooted down and positioned herself between Echo's legs. She dropped a tender kiss to Echo's thigh. "Even knowing what you do about Hyde and how he's treated you in the past, you are really going to go through with the mating?"

As much as she tried to resist, she needed to claim Echo. She could no longer fight it.

"I…I don't know," Echo whispered.

"You are my mate. As much as I tried to ignore the call, I can't," Mindi admitted. She dragged her fangs up Echo's inner thigh.

Echo stiffened.

"What did you just say?" Echo's voice was barely above a whisper.

"You are my mate. You belong to me."

Echo swallowed hard and pulled away. She scrambled from the bed, almost falling to the floor.

Mindi pushed up from the bed, confused. She slid to the side of the bed, unsure of what she'd said or done.

"I'm sorry," Echo hiccupped. She picked up her clothes and began throwing them on.

"What did I say?"

"Nothing." Echo froze in place and closed her eyes. "I mean, everything you said was perfect."

If everything she'd said was perfect, then why was Echo still getting dressed? Mindi stood from the bed and moved over to Echo. She grabbed her wrist and held her still.

"Then what is the matter? What's got you so spooked?"

Big fat tears welled up in Echo's eyes. Panic began to set inside Mindi. She didn't like to see Echo cry and was willing to do whatever she had to do to take them away. She reached up and gently wiped them away as they spilled onto Echo's cheeks. "Talk to me, baby. What is it?"

Echo inhaled sharply. She pulled away from Mindi, shaking her head.

Instantly, Mindi's wolf went on alert. Echo drawing back away from her couldn't be good. Had her wolf been wrong? Did Echo not feel what Mindi was feeling?

"You asked me if I was going to still go through with mating Hyde. Honestly, I don't want to." Echo reached up and angrily wiped the wetness from her face with the backs of her hands. "And as much as I loved hearing that your wolf recognized me as your mate, I can't do anything about it."

"What? Why not?" Mindi's anxiety was going through the roof. If Echo felt the same and her bear recognized Mindi as her mate, there was something she could do. Ditch Hyde and mate with Mindi.

"According to clan laws, a bear can only mate with a bear."

Echo's words cut through Mindi like a knife. She took a step back, pain like nothing she'd ever experienced ripping through her. She had never heard of such a thing.

Bear for bear?

Not following fate's path in life was preposterous. Mindi had tried to push the call to mate with Echo aside, but ultimately, she knew she wouldn't be able to win.

All shifters followed what fate had in store for them.

The call to mate with the one designed for you was no different than breathing.

It was necessary in order to live.

"What are you saying?" Mindi asked.

"I don't know," Echo whispered. She pushed her dark hair behind her ear. She wrung her hands together. "I need more time. Please understand. I want everything with you, but I just can't right now."

Echo spun on her heel and raced toward the stairs. Mindi followed behind her in disbelief. Echo opened the side door and whirled around toward Mindi.

Mindi stood in the doorway, uncaring that she was still naked. Her focus was on Echo at the moment.

"Echo," Mindi began, but Echo held a hand up.

"Just give me time. Please." Echo jogged down the short walkway toward the street. She disappeared around the corner.

Mindi leaned against the doorjamb, unsure of what to do.

Her animal snarled.

The wolf in her wasn't going to let her sit back. Her beast was headstrong, and they were going to fight for their mate.

She just had to figure out how.

"Here's your Diet Coke, my dear." Barb arrived at the table and set Mindi's glass down. "And I found your friend."

Mindi smiled at Marley who slid into the booth across from her.

"Thanks, Barb." Marley shot the older woman a smile. "I'll take the same thing."

"Coming right up." Barb grinned. She waved to the both of them. "Hurry up and glance at the menu. There's a few new items."

"Yes, ma'am," they both echoed.

Mindi grinned at her longtime friend. They had grown up together. Marley was the daughter of the alpha, Evan. Their fathers were best friends and considered each other as a brother. Their friendship dated back to when the men were pups. It was only natural for Evan to choose Mick as his beta when he took over the pack when his father retired.

Mindi had reached out to Marley to discuss her certain problem.

Echo's clan not accepting outsiders as mates.

Marley had briefly encountered that with her mate. Her best friend, Zara, was identified by Marley's wolf as her mate. But Marley had chosen to not say anything because her friend was human and had only dated men. It wasn't until they had gone on a boating trip that went wrong where their true feelings came out.

Mindi remembered how frantic her father and the alpha had been when the girls had gone missing. Lucky enough, Marley's survival skills kicked in and she was able to protect her mate.

Once they were home, Zara's father had gone berserk and had forbidden Zara from seeing Marley.

Hence why Mindi needed to speak with Marley. She needed advice on getting Echo's clan to accept her, a wolf, mating with Echo, a bear.

"It's so good to see you." Marley smiled. "It's been forever since I've seen or heard from you."

"Sorry about that." Mindi grinned sheepishly.

"I've been busy with work. My schedule has been filled, and I'm now booked out months in advance."

"That's awesome."

"Here, give this to your mom, will you." Mindi pushed a sealed manilla envelope to her. Jena Gerwulf had commissioned Mindi for a boudoir photo shoot. "You may not want to open it. Just give it to your mom."

"Oh, don't tell me she had you—" Marley grimaced and held up a hand. "Never mind. Don't tell me."

Mindi laughed at her friend's expression. Her mother was a beautiful woman who wanted to feel sexy. That was the point of her boudoir shoots. To empower a woman and bring out her inner goddess.

"Your mom had fun, and that's what those shoots are for." Mindi reached for her glass and took a sip.

They began looking over the new menu so they could order when Barb returned. Mindi didn't miss Marley's muttering that her mom was too old for those types of pictures.

Mindi laughed even harder. Wolves did not age like humans, and Marley's mom didn't look a day over forty.

Barb brought over Marley's Coke and took their orders. She disappeared with the promise to return soon.

"Okay, so I know you didn't have me meet you for lunch just to give me that." Marley pointed at the envelope. "You could have just dropped those off at their house."

"No, that is not the reason why we're having lunch." Mindi nervously played with her glass. She didn't know any other way to approach the subject without just blurting it out. "I found my mate."

Marley's eyebrows rose high. She let out a low whistle and clapped.

"Wow. I didn't see that coming," Marley said. "I thought you were against mating and wanted to live the playgirl life for a while."

"I did, but that was before I met her." Mindi couldn't help the smile that played on her lips.

"I'm happy for you." Marley giggled and reached out a hand and laid it on top of Mindi's.

"Thanks." Mindi sighed. She glanced up and met Marley's eyes, her smile disappearing. "But there's a problem. She's a bear shifter who is being forced into an arranged mating."

"Oh, snap." Marley's smile faded. "Oh, I'm so

sorry. I heard bear shifters forbid their bears from mating outside."

"She didn't tell me until recently." How the hell did Marley know that, but she didn't? Did Mindi miss a class or a lesson in shifter mating practice when she was younger? Was this common knowledge? "What can I do? It's fate. We are meant to be. My wolf knows it, her bear knows it."

"Fight for her." Marley's wolf rumbled. Her amber eyes locked on Mindi. "You are a strong wolf, the daughter of a beta. Prove to her that fate didn't get you two wrong and that you would face anything for her."

"I would," Mindi automatically replied. There was no question about it. She was a strong wolf and would be willing to face anyone who would defy fate.

"If you need anything, I'm here for you."

"Thanks, Marley."

Barb returned to their table with their food. Mindi would need sustenance in order to plan a way to win the right to complete the mating bond with Echo.

CHAPTER ELEVEN

Echo shut off her car and sat staring at her childhood home. She rubbed her sweaty hands on her jeans and exhaled sharply.

"We can do this." Her bear's ears twitched, but she didn't make any move to stand. Echo rolled her eyes. Of all days she needed to pull strength from her animal, the lazy bear just lay there. "Seriously? No help?"

Her animal snorted.

"Ugh!" Echo snatched the handle to her car and exited the vehicle. She closed the door and walked to the house. She reached up and tucked her dark hair behind her ear. She went up on the porch and rang the doorbell. Opening the door, she hesitantly stepped inside. The sound of her father making his way to the front of the house could be heard. "Dad?"

"Whatcha ringing the doorbell for? This is still your home, girl." Her father's voice was rough. There was a playful glint in his eyes.

"I just didn't want to startle you. I didn't know if you had a lady friend over." She shrugged, shutting the screen behind her.

"You know there is no other woman for me other than your mother." His cheeks grew red.

"Well, it's time you found a woman." She tilted her chin up in the air. Little did he know she was still determined to find someone for him. She had sent a text to her brothers the other night with the idea, and they both were on board. They had made a dinner date to discuss details.

"Please. No one wants an old bear like me." He waved her toward the door. "Come on. Let's go sit outside. I was headed that way."

They went out onto the porch and over to the large wooden rockers. Echo took a seat next to her father. They sat in a comfortable silence, staring out onto the land that had been in their family for years. Their property was large enough where she and her brothers all had their own cabins built on Norden land. They were far enough away to have privacy, but not too far away from each other.

The fluttering in Echo's stomach grew as she thought about the conversation she was about to approach with her father.

She gently rocked in the chair, enjoying the weather they were having. She glanced over at her father who was gazing at nature.

"What's got you so nervous, baby?" he asked, breaking the silence. Of course, he would pick up on her emotions. "I'm sure you came over here for something other than to sit and spend time with your old man."

"Dad..." She blew out a nervous breath. He always tried to claim he was old, but he was in the prime of his life. He was as healthy as a bear could be. "You're right. I did come over to speak with you about something important."

"I've told you and your brothers since you were cubs that you can always come and speak with me about anything." He glanced at her with wisdom gleaming in his eyes. He reached out and patted her on her knee. "I love you. Right now, when I look at you, all I see is your mother. Goddess rest her soul."

Echo smiled, trying to hold back her tears. Her mother had been taken from them in a freak accident. She had gone to the city visiting with girl-friends. There was a thick forest fire raging that had dense smoke filling the air. It had grown late, and Rovel had insisted Zottie stay overnight in the city, but her stubborn mother wanted to get home to her mate and cubs.

She'd left anyway and was headed home when she caught a flat tire. With the forest fire getting worse, the visibility was poor. Zottie had gotten out of her car to check on the tire and was hit by a drunken driver. The impact had killed her almost immediately.

Not even shifters could survive something like that.

"She was beautiful," Echo murmured. They kept all of the pictures of her mother throughout the house. Even though she had been gone for a long time, a day didn't go by that Echo didn't think of her.

When she'd died, Echo had tried to help out as much as she could. She had learned to cook at her mother's hip and continued on ensuring her father had food to eat. In the weeks and months following his mate's death, her father had stopped taking care of himself. If it hadn't been for her and her brothers, he would have wasted away and joined Zottie in the afterlife.

But he had cubs depending on him. It was hard for him to move on, but he did it for the three of them.

"Now, tell me, child. What is it?" He gave her knee another squeeze then lifted his hand.

"I can't go through this mating with Hyde."

"Not this again, Echo." He glided his fingers through his dark hair. He glanced away momentarily before turning back to her.

"I'm serious, Daddy." She switched on her big brown cub eyes she would use when she was a kid. It had worked on him every single time.

"Why? What is the reason you cannot mate with Hyde?" Her father grew exasperated. "He's from a respectable family. Sure, he's an ass and a little rough around the edges, but what male bear isn't?"

She took her father's large hand in hers and threaded their fingers together. She remained calm and hoped her energy went over to him.

"I've found my true mate, Daddy," she said softly.

Rovel froze in place. His same brown eyes she'd

inherited, widened in shock. His mouth moved a few times, opening and closing, but no words had come out.

She'd stumped the old man.

He blinked, and then a smile spread across his face.

"Well, I'll be damned." He slapped his leg. Excitement lined his face. "Baby, that is fantastic. Who is it? I'm sure that with this knowledge that it's your true mate, we will be able to break off the arrangement."

Echo prayed that this would be true once she told him who fate had designed for her.

"It's Mindi. Do you remember the beta of the Nightstar Pack? His daughter is my fated mate."

"Impossible." Rovel froze.

"No, it's not impossible." She shook her head and tightened her grip on his hand. She had to make him believe what she was saying or there was no hope in her getting out of the arrangement with Hyde. "Before I even met her, my bear knew my mate was in the house. When I laid eyes on her, my bear was uncontrollable. I've had to fight my bear to keep from claiming her."

Big fat tears rolled down her cheeks.

"Are you for certain?" he asked.

"Fate has determined that my mate is a wolf not a bear." It felt so good to get that off her chest. She had accepted it immediately, but saying it aloud to her father was different. If he didn't side with her, then she would have to go with plan B, and that would be to defy him and the entire clan. She would be an outcast, but following fate was worth it.

Mindi was worth it.

Echo had begged Mindi for more time, and she was going to go back to her mate to claim her with or without the blessing of her family and clan.

"That's not going to sit right with the clan. You know the rules, Echo."

"Are we better than fate and the goddess above? Who are we to defy what fate has planned for any of us?" She hopped up from her chair and faced her father with her hands resting on her waist. Her bear growled in agreement.

Oh, now you want to chime in.

Her father stood from his chair and stopped in front of her. He placed his hands on her shoulders.

"Baby, all I have ever wanted in life was to be the best father I could. But if I don't trust in fate and side with you, then I would be a horrible father and would fail you." He squeezed her and brought her in for a tight hug. "Failing you is not an option.

Your mother would have my hide if I didn't trust in you and fate."

"Daddy, what are you saying?" She pulled back to look him in the eye. Hope flared inside her.

"I'm saying that we will have to go and speak with my brother. There hasn't been a mating between a bear and a wolf around these parts that I'm aware of."

"What about Bubba and Naomi? They were allowed to mate, and Naomi is human." Echo was desperate to make her plea. There had been an exception here and there along the years.

Bubba and Naomi Clancy were mated years ago and had children. Of their four kids, all of them were bear shifters. If the council was worried about offspring, then there was no way they would have known the Clancy brood would have been born shifters. Echo had always heard it was a fifty-fifty chance when it came to shifter and human couplings.

"You're right, baby. Come, let's go pay a visit to my brother."

Echo exited her father's truck and walked around the hood to join him. Butterflies filled her belly.

"Don't worry. Your uncle will hear us out." Her father patted her on the back and motioned for her to go with him.

The sound of an ax striking wood sounded from behind the alpha's house. They followed the sound into the wooded area until they came upon Trion splitting logs.

Her uncle, a great grizzly, would have had no trouble cutting the tree down on his own.

He glanced up as they approached him.

"What do I owe the pleasure of having my favorite brother and favorite niece come visit?" A smile spread across his face.

"I'm your only niece," Echo grumbled playfully.

He tossed her a wink and focused on Rovel.

"And I'm your only brother." Her father chuckled.

"Either way, know that you're loved and appreciated." He tossed the ax down on the ground and mopped his forehead with the back of his hand.

He must have been at this for a while because the pile of freshly cut logs was staggering.

"You should have called. I would have come and helped you," Rovel said.

"I don't need help." Trion snorted. He picked up a piece of wood and split it in two with his bare hands.

"Show-off." Her father folded his arms in front of him. He glanced over at Echo then faced Trion.

"I sense this is more than just a family visit?" Trion took a seat on a stump and reached for his towel and water canteen. He wiped the towel around his face, head, and neck, resting it on his shoulders.

"Yes, we need to talk."

Echo's heartbeat thundered in her ears. She could barely hear what her father said. Worry filled her. What if her uncle would not honor fate's decision? What if he wanted her to still mate with Hyde?

Echo dried her clammy hands on her jeans and focused on her father and uncle.

Trion took a long gulp of his water and eyed them.

"What's the problem?" he asked, sitting the canteen down on the ground.

"We're here to speak with you about Echo and Hyde's arrangement," her father announced.

A scowl immediately appeared on Trion's face.

Rovel held his hand out. "You really need to hear this."

Rovel motioned to her.

Echo blew out a shaky breath and stood to her full height.

"I cannot mate with Hyde, Uncle Trion." Echo took a step forward. She didn't know where this strength was coming from, but she was going to make her point and convince him to let her out of the arrangement.

"I know there was some bad blood between you and he when you were children, Echo. That's all in the past—"

"I've found my true mate," she blurted out.

Trion paused and stared at her. He stood to his full height and ambled over to her. Echo tilted her head back to meet her uncle's gaze. He was extremely tall and towered over her. He reached out a hand and cupped her chin, moving her head side to side.

"Where's your claiming mark?"

"Because of the agreement between our family and Hyde's, I've resisted," she admitted. Tears filled her eyes. "It has been the hardest thing I have ever experienced, uncle. My bear is confused on why I haven't acted on it. She's going nuts."

"And the bear who is your mate—"

"Is not a bear," Rovel interjected.

"Not a bear!" Her uncle's voice thundered, echoing around them.

She cringed and stepped back. She bit her lip, worried.

"What do you mean your mate is not a bear?"

"This is fate, uncle." She lowered her eyes in respect. Her uncle's bear was near the surface, and hers lay down, submitting to the stronger animal. "Never in a million years would I have thought that fate would have determined the person I was to spend my entire life with would be a wolf."

"And you are sure its fate?" Trion questioned.

Her father stood next to her and rested a hand on her shoulder. She glanced up and met her uncle's stare.

"As sure as I'm a bear."

Trion shoved a hand through his hair and blew out a deep breath. He took a few steps away from them.

Her father gave her a comforting nod.

Trion spun around on his heel and faced her.

"Mating outside of our kind hasn't been done

that often," Trion began. He walked back to them and stopped in front of Echo. "I will speak with the council, and the contract will be voided. I will not be an alpha who stands in the way of fate. That's not how I will have the Brokenclaw viewed."

Echo threw herself at Trion. Her burly uncle wrapped his arms around her and gave a squeeze.

"Thank you," she sniffed, tears blearing her vision.

"Don't worry about a thing. I will take care of this, niece." Trion's large hand stroked her hair. "It will be tough to go against the council, but you are my blood, and I won't have anything stand in the way of you claiming your mate.'

Echo glanced over at her father who was standing near them with a smile on his face.

Echo sighed, feeling excited that she was going to be able to claim her woman.

CHAPTER TWELVE

M indi blew out a deep breath and guided her car up the winding road of the mountain. Echo had called her and invited Mindi to her home.

Mindi grew nervous, unsure what Echo would say once she got there.

She had never been in a committed relationship before. This was new territory for her. She'd always kept everything casual between her and lovers.

Just give me time. Please.

Echo's voice sounded in her head.

Things between them were left in limbo. It had

been a few days since Echo had practically raced from her house. Mindi dove into work to stay busy. Thinking of the fear and doubt that had been in Echo's eyes was driving her crazy. She just wanted to rush out and find Echo and hold her in her arms.

But she hadn't.

Mindi tried to remain patient while she gave Echo time as she'd asked. Everything had been going fine until the second Mindi admitted she was giving in to her animal and fate and Echo appeared to freak the hell out.

It had left Mindi baffled. Her lunch with Marley had helped drastically.

One thing she took away from speaking with her old friend was to let nature take its course. Marley had waited forever, and everything had worked out for her and Zara. They were now a happily mated couple.

Mindi sat up straighter in her seat, trying to boost her own confidence.

Prove to her that fate didn't get you two wrong and that you would face anything for her.

Mindi's wolf snarled. She was a strong wolf. Mindi was willing to do whatever she had to do to prove that she was good enough for a bear shifter.

Her hand tightened on the steering wheel. She

guided the car onto the road that led to Echo's home.

Her wolf paced the closer to she got to Echo.

Soon, Mindi arrived at the cabin. It was a beautiful home tucked away in the dense forest. It had everything a single bear shifter would want. The picturesque landscape with plush bushes and flower gardens surrounded the building. The navy-blue shutters stood out against the white paint of the siding.

The cozy cabin fit Echo.

Mindi killed the engine and stared at the place. She pushed down her nervousness. There was a reason Echo had called and invited her up here. It was time for her to go find out.

She exited the car and stood next to it, breathing in the delicious aroma of barbecue. Mindi's stomach rumbled.

Following the scent, Mindi strolled around to the back and found Echo standing at the grill.

"Something smells wonderful," Mindi announced.

"You made it!" Echo spun around with a grin plastered on her lips.

One look at Echo, and Mindi's nerves melted away.

"Of course I would come. Did you have any doubt I wouldn't?" Mindi walked onto the patio and made her way to Echo.

"I knew you would come," Echo murmured.

"There's not anything that would keep me away from you." Mindi arrived next to Echo and opened her arms.

Echo stepped into them and wrapped hers around Mindi.

"That's good to hear." Echo lifted her face to Mindi and offered her lips.

Mindi covered them with hers in a deep, passionate kiss. It had been a few days since she had held her in her arms, and Mindi couldn't help but take advantage of this moment. Her tongue slipped inside Echo's mouth and stroked hers.

Mindi gently released Echo and rested her forehead on Echo's. She inhaled the scent of her mate. Her wolf prowled around, wanting more.

"You came in time. I just finished preparing dinner." Echo smiled and took hold of Mindi's hand. She tugged Mindi behind her and guided her over to the table that was set for two. "Please have a seat."

Echo brimmed with excitement. Mindi was curious as to what she had to share with her, but it would appear Echo had gone all out and Mindi would just have to learn patience. She didn't want to ruin what Echo had planned by demanding to know what was going on.

So instead, she sat back and waited.

"Are you sure you don't need me to help?" Mindi asked. She watched Echo step over to the grill.

"I'm sure. I'm just going to make our plates, then we can talk." Echo tossed a grin over her shoulder. She pointed to the wine on the table. "You can open the wine and pour our glasses."

"Sure." Mindi took the glasses. She opened the bottle and filled them up.

Echo returned to the table with two plates crammed with food.

Mindi's stomach rumbled again from the aroma of the food. She hadn't realized how hungry she was.

"I hope surf and turf is okay." Echo took the seat next to Mindi. Both plates were piled high with steaks, grilled salmon, and sides.

"This looks amazing," Mindi exclaimed.

"We have desserts, too, but those are for later." There was a mischievous gleam in her eye. She reached for her glass and held it up in the air. "Mind if I do a toast?"

"Sure." Mindi shrugged.

"To us," Echo said softly.

Mindi froze, her glass in the air. She studied Echo's eyes, trying to see the underlying meaning.

"Are you saying what I think you are saying?" Excitement grew in Mindi's chest.

Echo nodded, her smile spreading wide.

"My uncle will speak with the council. As the alpha, he can't turn his back on fate." Echo took Mindi's hand. "So, to us, fate, and new beginnings."

"Hear, hear." Mindi touched her glass to Echo's. She squeezed her hand and took a sip of the wine. It was a nice red that would pair well with the large steak on her plate. The wolf inside her was licking her chops. "I'm so happy to hear this."

"We have lots to plan, but first, I think after we eat, we should allow our animals to meet."

"That would be a great idea." Mindi's wolf was dying to meet Echo's bear. She could sense the other animal, but it was nothing like meeting in person. A run in the woods with her mate would be a great way for their animals to get to know each other.

Mindi was enjoying her dinner with her mate.

Echo had certainly impressed Mindi with her cooking. She knew the bear shifter owned a bakery, but the food was phenomenal. She couldn't eat it fast enough to satisfy her wolf.

They had the perfect backdrop of the woods with the melody of nature as the soundtrack. Nighttime had fallen. Large solar-powered LED lanterns were placed around the patio and cast soft light around them. Mindi could barely take her eyes off Echo. She was so beautiful. Her smile was infectious, and her laugh was musical.

Echo shared with Mindi her conversation with her father and uncle. Mindi was in shock that it didn't take much to convince them. Bears were notoriously known to be stubborn, but it would appear that even they wouldn't go against fate.

Mindi began thinking of planning for Echo to come and meet her family. They would be welcoming to Echo.

"I want you to come meet my family," Mindi blurted out.

"I would love that." Echo grinned at her. She had been all smiles and relaxed as if a weight had been removed from her shoulders.

Mindi was happy that it would appear they would be able to act on what was between them.

They could begin planning their future together and the mating.

"Good." Apprehension filled Mindi slightly. Her parents knew how she felt about mating. They were going to be surprised when she brought Echo home to introduce her as her mate.

Mindi's eyes dropped down to Echo's shoulder. Echo wore a little sexy dress that exposed both of her shoulders. She couldn't wait to sink her fangs into the soft flesh and mark Echo has hers forever.

They finished their meal and cleared the table together. Mindi followed Echo into her home and helped put away the food and rinse the dishes and put them in the dishwasher.

"Come." Echo took Mindi's hand and led her back outside.

They walked to the edge of the patio.

Echo turned and backed away from Mindi with a cute grin on her face. "My bear has been wanting to be let out since you arrived."

Mindi's breath caught in her throat at the sight of Echo tugging her dress over her head. Her bra and panties did little to cover her.

"Is that so?" Mindi reached for her clothes and began taking them off. She made her way over to Echo, unable to keep her hands off the tantalizing curves of her mate. Mindi nuzzled Echo's neck, dropping soft kisses to the area she vowed to place her mark. Echo's hands slid down Mindi's torso and around to her ass.

A growl ripped from Mindi at the sensation of her mate's body pressing against hers. She reached up behind Echo and undid her bra, dropping it onto the ground. Echo made easy work of Mindi's, allowing hers to fall into a pile.

Echo's giggles filled the air as they made it farther into the yard. She backed away from Mindi and spun around.

"Where you going?" Mindi rasped. She wasn't ready to let Echo go.

"We're supposed to be introducing our animals." Echo did a seductive dance, shaking her ass for Mindi. She pushed her panties down and bent over on purpose, exposing herself. "You keep that up and we'll miss out on our run."

"We have plenty of time to go for a run." Mindi's heart raced. She got rid of hers, leaving her naked.

"No. My bear wants to finally meet you." Echo took another step back; dark fur sprouted from her creamy skin.

Mindi paused, watching her mate going

through the change. It was a beautiful sight to see her mate contorting into her beast.

Who would have thought a bear and a wolf would be fated together?

Not Mindi, but she had no doubt that fate knew what she was doing.

Mindi had a feeling that nothing would ever be dull between her and Echo.

Mindi's wolf howled, scratching to be released. Her animal was desperate to get to their mate.

Mindi gave in to her wolf's demands, allowing her to take over. Her black fur appeared. Her gums stretched and burned from her fangs dropping down. She fell to her knees, her bones stretching and reconfiguring into her animal.

She closed her eyes, allowing her wolf to come forward. Mindi opened them seconds later and found a large six-hundred-pound grizzly waiting for her.

Echo.

Mindi stared at her mate in her animal form and didn't feel an ounce of fear. They gazed at each other as if wanting to memorize the other.

They stepped forward, sniffing hesitantly at first.

Mindi pressed her face into Echo's fur and inhaled sharply. She backed away, allowing Echo to take her turn. The bear's snout nudged Mindi's neck. She breathed in, taking Mindi's scent in.

They moved from each other, not breaking their stare.

Mindi gave a yip and rushed toward the forest. Her wolf was feeling playful and wanted to be chased by her bear.

She paused and glanced over her shoulder. Echo gave a roar, standing on her hind legs. A grin overtook the bear's lips. She fell back down to all four legs and raced after Mindi.

She turned and raced into the woods with her mate hot on her tail. The ground shook as Echo caught up to her.

Her wolf grinned, finally satisfied to be around her mate.

They took off deep in the woods as a couple. Animals of the forest scurried away from the threat of two hunters in the area. Their animals played and teased each other.

Mindi had never experienced such happiness before.

Nothing could make this day be any better.

CHAPTER THIRTEEN

Echo's bear was at peace. They had scampered around with Mindi for what seemed like hours. She snuggled into the warmth of Mindi's embrace. They lay on a patch of thick grass, staring up at the moon.

Her bear was in love with Mindi's wolf. The two animals had got along like they were an old married couple. The two were a match made in Heaven.

Echo adjusted her head and stared at the dark sky.

"Did you see that?" Mindi raised her hand and pointed to a shooting star.

"We have to make a wish." Echo closed her eyes and immediately knew what she wanted to wish for.

I wish to claim my mate.

She ached to sink her fangs into Mindi's flesh and mark her for all eternity. There would be no other for her.

Mindi was it.

Echo opened her eyes and found Mindi staring at her.

"Did you make your wish?" Echo asked.

"I did." Mindi nodded. "What did you wish for?"

"I can't tell you." Echo grinned and tapped Mindi on her nose. "It's bad luck to share what you wish for, and it won't come true."

"Is that so?" Mindi's eyebrows rose sharply.

"Well, at least that's what my mother used to say." Echo's smile slowly faded as she thought of her mother. She missed her fiercely. Zottie Norden would have loved Mindi, and she would have fought tooth and nail to ensure Echo would be able to complete her mating with her wolf. There were times Echo sat under the stars and wondered if her mother was looking down on her. She pretended that she was and talked with her mother's spirit.

Being the only female in a house full of

rambunctious male bears was so hard. None of them understood what it was like to be a female.

She'd stayed the night at her uncle's home so she could spend time with Dari, her cousin, just to have a female to speak with.

"Tell me about your mother." Mindi's fingers slowly stroked the side of Echo's cheek.

"My father always says I look just like her," Echo began after a moment. She blew out a deep breath and glanced at the stars as if to check if her mother was listening. It was a hard habit to break. She was sure Zottie watched over her while she grew up. "She was a stubborn woman who knew how to rein in my father and brothers. She taught me everything I know about cooking and baking."

"Well, I wish I could thank her." Mindi pressed a chaste kiss to Echo's lips.

"We would spend hours in the kitchen baking. It was my favorite thing to do. I loved trialing new recipes. She would ensure I had what I needed. I remember I baked my first cake at the age of seven. It was a mess, but it was so good."

Echo smiled, remembering the expression on her father's face. He had taken everything in stride, tasting the cake and shouting how good it was. It had to be one of the ugliest cakes ever produced, but her father, after a stern glare from her mother, had praised it to be the best one he'd ever eaten.

"I'm sure she would be proud of your bakery and the woman you have become," Mindi said.

"I know she would have." Echo drew a finger down Mindi's sternum. "She would have adored you."

"Really?"

"Yes, she had a love of the arts, too. The weekend she was killed, her and her friends had gone into the city to see some new art exhibit that was at the museum. It was a weekend away. The perfect girls' weekend for women who loved wine and art."

"Certainly my kind of lady." Mindi smiled and brushed Echo's thick tresses from her face.

Echo's smile disappeared as she shared with Mindi the tragic demise of her mother. It still brought tears to her eyes to think of her death. Her father had assured her and her brothers that Zottie hadn't suffered.

All these years later, Echo believed her mother was in the heavens watching over them. Glancing up at the moon, Echo felt a tug at her heart.

Yes, her mother's spirit was nearby.

She smiled, a warming sensation coming over them.

"I wish you could have met her." Echo kissed Mindi. It was a slow kiss. Their lips molded to each other in a tantalizing dance. She poured all of her emotions into the kiss.

Knowing that she was free to mate with the woman she loved—

Echo sighed. Yes, she knew without a doubt that what she felt for Mindi was love.

She pulled back from Mindi, her breaths coming fast. She stared into Mindi's amber eyes and suddenly felt the overwhelming need to share what she was feeling.

"Even though fate brought us together, I'm falling in love with you." Echo's heart skipped a beat. She bit her lip, unsure if this was too soon. Mindi's amber eyes were locked on her. Echo panicked slightly. "You don't have to reciprocate. I know this is new for us, but I wanted to share with you."

Echo felt more free, sexy, and open about her feelings, all because of this woman. No matter what, she meant what she'd said, and Mindi was going to have to deal with it.

"I think I'm falling in love with you, too," Mindi

murmured. She rolled them over to where Echo was lying flat on her back. Mindi braced herself over her. She slowly blazed a trail of hot, open-mouthed kissed on Echo's body.

"Mindi," Echo gasped.

Her mate latched on to her nipple and suckled it deep into her mouth. Echo moaned, threading her fingers into Mindi's hair. She held her lover in place and arched her back up to offer more of herself to Mindi.

Her core clenched with need as Mindi took her time tasting Echo's breasts. Under her manipulation, Echo's nipples became even harder. Her pussy grew wet with Mindi's attention to her breasts.

Echo's body writhed on the plush grass.

Mindi released her one mound and turned her attention to the other one. The scent of their arousal filled the air. Echo breathed in the sweet smell of the proof of their need.

Mindi lifted her head and kissed Echo's lips. The kiss turned feral and deep. Echo skated her hand over Mindi's toned body. She rolled them to their sides where they lay facing each other.

Echo dove her hand between Mindi's legs, and she found her swollen bud. She focused her full attention on driving her mate crazy.

"Echo," Mindi groaned, her legs parting more.

Echo took advantage of the move and strummed Mindi's clit.

"That feels so good."

Mindi's hand slipped between Echo's thighs. She found Echo's clit and teased her. Her fingers massaged the swollen bud, eliciting a moan from Echo.

The kiss grew frantic. Echo suckled on Mindi's tongue, stroking it with hers.

Her hands were coated in Mindi's juices. She slid her fingers through Mindi's slick folds, collecting more of her honey. The warmth of Mindi's core was calling her. She wanted to dip her fingers inside the drenched channel and feel Mindi clench around her fingers.

Echo's heartbeat thundered in her ears. Her body overheated from the desire swimming through her. Mindi's fingers were working her toward a sweet climax. She gasped, breaking the kiss. Mindi applied pressure to her bud while trailing hot kisses on Echo's cheeks, down to her neck.

Echo brought her fingers back to Mindi's little bundle of nerves. Their moans filled the air. Echo rubbed herself against Mindi, needing to feel her mate's soft skin.

"I need to feel your pussy against mine," Mindi muttered.

Her amber eyes were glowing with an intensity that took Echo's breath away.

Echo withdrew her fingers and brought them to her lips. She sucked them into her mouth, licking the cream from them. Mindi's eyes darkened as she watched.

She pushed Echo on to her back, with a growl escaping her lips.

"That was so sexy," Mindi murmured. She mimicked Echo. She cleaned her lover's honey from her fingers.

Mindi rose and braced herself over Echo. She parted her legs for Mindi to straddle her. Echo reached between them and spread her labia wide to allow her clit to be exposed. Mindi settled her pussy onto Echo's, lining her clit up with hers.

"Oh God," Echo breathed. Her swollen nub was sensitive and slick. It wasn't going to take much for her to reach that euphoric journey.

"Fuck, this feels so good." Mindi's eyes closed while she rocked her hips.

Echo held on to her waist to help guide her. She spread her legs wider, needing to feel more of

Mindi on her. Echo's hand remained between them, keeping her labia open.

A shudder went through her at the sensations of their slick pussies sliding against each other. Echo's gaze was locked on the sight of Mindi's swinging breasts. The perky nipples were teasing her. Mindi rested her hands on the ground on either side of Echo's head, bringing those beautiful breasts close enough for Echo to capture with her mouth.

She closed her lips around the first nipple, eliciting a shout from Mindi. She teased the hard bud with her tongue.

Their movements grew more frantic.

Echo's heart raced; her breaths were coming faster.

Their hips rocked together in unison. Echo dug her fingers into Mindi's flesh. Waves of ecstasy washed over Echo. She teetered on the edge of the unbelievable pleasure that coursed through her body.

Mindi pumped her hips faster. They writhed against each other, until finally they reached their orgasms together.

Their cries cut through the air.

Echo didn't care who or what heard them. She wrapped her arms around Mindi and pulled her down to her. They lay flush until their breaths slowed down to a steady rhythm.

She closed her eyes and inhaled Mindi's intoxicating scent. Her bear let out a pleased rumble. She was happy Mindi was here, but her bear wanted more.

Mindi was hers to claim, and her animal was ready to do what was needed to mark Mindi as hers forever.

CHAPTER FOURTEEN

Mindi tightened her grip on Echo's hand and stole a glance at her mate. Letting their animals out to roam and play with each other was a great idea.

Mindi's wolf was excited to meet their mate. It didn't matter that Echo was a bear. Her wolf was enthralled by the oversized shifter.

They were strolling through the woods, heading back to Echo's home. Mindi tugged Echo to her, needing to feel her soft curves against her.

"Tonight, was perfect," Mindi murmured. She curled her arm around Echo's waist.

Echo turned to her with a wide grin. "It was."

Her wolf sat up, confused as to why they hadn't claimed Echo in the woods. They had plenty of opportunities while they'd made love.

But that was the thing.

Mindi couldn't keep her hands off Echo long enough to sink her fangs into her. She had been too busy devouring what was between Echo's thighs.

The multiple orgasm was addictive, too. Mindi stopped counting after the third one.

Mindi gazed at the beautiful night sky. There were millions of tiny stars littering the dark backdrop.

Their time in the woods had been magical. Mindi wasn't sure if it was the mating bond growing between them or what, but she really was eager to mate with Echo.

She hadn't expected to find her mate at this point in her life, but now that she had, she couldn't wait for their life together.

"What are you thinking about?" Mindi peeked over at Echo. The bear had a silly grin on her face. Mindi's hand skated across her soft skin and cupped her ass.

They stepped out of the woods and began walking up to Echo's house. The cabin sat undisturbed, and Mindi looked forward to setting in for the night with Echo.

"Well, I was wondering if you would spend the night." Echo shrugged.

"There's no way I'm leaving tonight." Mindi leaned over and dropped a kiss on Echo's lips.

"Good." Echo spun toward Mindi and wrapped her arms around her neck. Their kiss deepened.

Mindi's heart raced. The feeling of Echo's voluptuous body was turning her on. The scent of Echo's arousal reached Mindi's nose. Her wolf growled.

Claim her.

It was time.

Mindi broke the kiss and took Echo by her hand. They rushed toward the back porch. Mindi's gaze landed on an imposing figure standing on the steps.

They skated to a halt.

"I've been waiting for you to return home," Hyde growled. He stepped off the stair and paused, glaring at them.

"What are you doing here, Hyde?" Echo asked. Her muscles were tense. She tightened her hold on Mindi's hand.

They paused in the middle of the yard. Something didn't sit right with Mindi. There was no way they would go any closer to the bear. With her keen vision at night, she could make out the expression on Hyde's face.

Mindi sensed the angry vibes rolling off him. It didn't take a rocket scientist to see he was beyond pissed. She tensed, preparing for anything.

A pissed-off bear who was unpredictable was dangerous.

"The alpha came to me and my father and told me he was voiding our agreement." He turned his gaze to Mindi. His lips curled up into a snarl. A growl snaked its way from him. He appeared to grow in size as he huffed. He took a step toward them, his animal coming dangerously close to the surface. "A wolf. You are breaking up with me for a wolf?"

"We should have never been arranged. I didn't want to mate with you," Echo shouted. She released Mindi's hand. "You know you didn't want me. Nobody wanted me. Remember when you told me that? Here's your way out."

Mindi jerked back as if she were hit.

No one wanted Echo?

How could they not? What was wrong with

these bears? Were they blind? Echo was a beautiful woman and bear.

"It doesn't matter. Your family signed a contract. They should honor that." Hyde was losing control of himself. His fangs had descended, and little sprouts of fur had appeared on his arms.

He was about to shift.

Mindi blinked and moved closer to Echo.

"Echo," Mindi whispered fiercely.

Echo was on a roll and didn't realize what was happening in front of her.

"Mindi is my mate. We are going to claim each other, and you need to leave." Echo stomped her foot and pointed toward the front of the house.

Had this been any other time and a different situation, it would have been downright cute.

But they had a pissed-off grizzly who was about to shift and be in a rage.

And his attention was on Mindi.

She swallowed hard. This bear was gunning for her because of what fate had done.

Fate had chosen to pair a bear and a wolf.

She was standing between something his human side wanted.

It wasn't her fault, but he was going to take out his anger on her. Mindi was going to have to defend what she and Echo had. She was sure Hyde wasn't going to be the only person with an issue with a wolf and a bear mating.

"Like hell I'm leaving. She's mine, wolf." His final word was a growl. His fur continued to sprout from his skin. He began to shift, falling to the ground as his bones contorted.

"Shit." Mindi gave herself to her wolf. Her animal was on high alert, sensing the threat to her and her mate.

Mindi stood on all fours, and her attention was on the large eight-foot-tall, pissed-off grizzly.

Hyde roared.

Echo screamed, but Mindi didn't have time to check on her. Hyde fell down on his four legs and took off toward her.

She wouldn't be able to take on a grizzly his size. She did the only thing she could do.

Ran.

Mindi raced into the woods. There was no way she could afford to be captured by Hyde. The angry grizzly would tear her to shreds. Those massive claws would cut her in half. She was a large wolf but would be no match for him in his animal form.

The ground shook with Hyde hot on her tail. Bears were almost as fast as wolves. Mindi pushed herself faster. She leaped over a fallen tree and ran under the brush, trying to hide.

The sound of Hyde's roar wasn't far behind her. He burst through the tree stump as if it wasn't there.

Mindi skidded to a halt.

Dammit.

She'd made a wrong turn. She crept forward and glanced over the edge. There was a long drop that would take her down to the river.

She looked at the side of the hill; it was jagged with rocks. There was a slim chance she would survive the fall.

She was cornered.

Fierce growling sounded behind her. She spun around to the sight of Hyde advancing on her.

There was nothing for her to do but stand her ground.

Mindi bared her teeth, snarling at Hyde.

Her claws dug in the ground as her hackles rose. Her beast wasn't going to go down without a fight. Staring down a raging bear had Mindi's life flashing before her eyes.

Memories of her roughhousing with her brothers came to mind. Her parents celebrating her sixteenth birthday, surprising her with a car. Her first kiss.

The first time she'd laid eyes on Echo.

Their first night together.

A fierce growl ripped from Mindi. She would fight to the death to be able to spend all of eternity with the one person who was her other half.

Hyde advanced on her, leaving her no choice but to fight the oversized grizzly.

She raced toward him with her exposed fangs. She managed to escape the swipe of his massive paw. She darted in and was able to land a bite on his hind leg. Her teeth sank into him, and she held on. He jerked and roared.

The sound of Echo breaking through the brush stole Mindi's attention.

Large claws slashed through her side. The power of the hit sent her sprawling through the grass. She landed near the edge of the cliff. Her side burned, blood escaping the wound. The pain was excruciating. She released a howl, praying someone heard her.

It was a distress howl that any shifter should recognize.

Blood gushed from the wound, running down her side. She glanced up and saw Echo facing off with Hyde. She bravely stood on her hind legs, placing herself between Hyde and Mindi.

Mindi pushed up from the ground. She grimaced, trying to get her bearings. Her back right leg was practically useless.

Throwing back her head, she howled again. The sound carried off into the distance.

Someone had to answer her call.

She hopped slowly on three legs toward Echo. Her attention was locked on Hyde. Low growls rumbled through her. She came to stand next to Echo. They would face him together.

Hyde swung at Echo who dodged him and landed her own blow, gouging his chest with her claws.

Blood gushed from the wound, but it wasn't going to slow a bear like him down.

Mindi bared her teeth. She moved forward, intent on getting into the fight, but a weakness overcame her. She stumbled, her gaze going blurry.

Looked like she wasn't going to be any help at all.

Echo, she cried out in her mind, but her mate wouldn't be able to hear her.

Her knees gave out, and she toppled to the ground. Mindi tried with all of her strength to lift her head, but her neck wouldn't cooperate. Her limbs wouldn't follow any of her commands.

Her last thought was of Echo and how she'd failed her.

Then everything went black.

CHAPTER FIFTEEN

Out of the corner of her eye, Echo caught sight of Mindi crumbling to the ground.

Her bear roared, still standing on her hind legs. Her animal wanted to end Hyde. She was bloodthirsty for vengeance.

Echo would have been shocked any other day by the way her animal was reacting, but it was their mate.

Mindi was to be everything to her.

Pain rippled through her heart at the sight of an eerily still Mindi.

Echo turned her attention back to Hyde. He

was the cause of Mindi's wound. Her brave mate had tried to come and help but ended up on the receiving end of his deadly claws.

Hyde was distracted by Mindi. He made to move toward Mindi, but Echo stepped in front of her mate.

He would have to go through her to get to Mindi, and she was not going down without a fight. If he got past her, Mindi was as good as dead.

He blamed Mindi for her family breaking off the agreement. Had she not found her mate, Echo probably would have gone through with it.

But thanks to fate, her mate was given to her.

Now Echo was going to have to do everything in her power to save Mindi.

Echo rushed toward him, catching him off guard. Her claws sank into his chest. He roared, stepping back from her. Echo wasn't quick enough to dodge the paw that landed across her face. She stumbled back then went on the attack again.

She knew she wouldn't be a match against him, but she was willing to die to protect her mate.

She bared her teeth at him. Hyde backed away, issuing a warning huffing sound. She didn't care. It was life or death for Mindi.

A howl echoed off in the distance, followed by a roar.

Help was on the way.

Mindi had helped her before she had collapsed. That howl she let out must have been heard by someone.

Echo was tiring quickly, and she prayed whoever answered the call was close.

Echo wasn't sure how long she could keep up. She bellowed, warning Hyde away from her mate.

He advanced toward her, stomping his way to her on all fours.

Echo tried to push her fear down.

He drew close just when another form came crashing from the woods and barreled into Hyde.

Hyde and the newcomer crashed around on the ground. Their claws slashed through the air. Their growls grew louder.

Their movements were becoming a blur. She couldn't make out who the other bear was. Another bear emerged from the woods having heeded the call, and she now knew who was facing Hyde.

Her brothers, Vick and Cole.

She recognized Cole as he rushed toward the melee.

Vick was a savage when it came to fighting, and

the fact that it was she who was in danger, Hyde wasn't going to stand a chance against not just one brother but both.

Echo fell down on her four legs and rushed to Mindi. She used her snout to try to push her mate slightly to wake her.

Mindi was so still. Her side rose and fell steadily. The fur on her hip was matted with blood. Mindi had lost a lot. They were going to have to get her to a healer soon before she bled to death.

There was a rustling of the brush, and Echo glanced up. Two large wolves emerged. Their attention was at first drawn to the bear fight, but then they turned toward Echo and Mindi. They took one look at a still Mindi and bared their fangs.

Echo immediately pulled back on her beast, shifting back into her human form.

Her standing over a bloodied wolf didn't look good.

She fell to the ground, kneeling over Mindi's animal.

"Wait! It wasn't me," she gasped. Echo held her hands up. "Please. She's my mate and she needs help." She rested her head on Mindi's. Warm tears rolled down her cheeks. She buried her face into her thick fur.

The sounds of the bear fight quieted. Echo found the wolves creeping toward her.

Her gaze flicked over to where her brothers stood on their hind legs near the still form of Hyde.

Relief filled her that they had taken Hyde down. She didn't know if he was still alive, and at the moment, she didn't care.

"Is she breathing?" a deep voice asked.

Echo jerked, turning her attention to the large man before her. He knelt on the ground in front of Mindi.

"Yes," her voice quivered. She eyed him warily. In the back of her mind, she assumed since he was a wolf, he belonged to Mindi's pack.

"My name is Jatix," he murmured. He ran his hand over Mindi's body and paused at her wound. "I'm an enforcer for the Nightstar."

Echo nodded. Her bear didn't like the fact he was putting his hand on her mate. She pushed down the urge to growl at him.

He is here to help.

Her bear whined and plopped down.

"We need to get her to a healer," Echo whispered. Mindi had lost a lot of blood. She glanced over and saw a few other bears had arrived.

The calvary was finally there.

The clan's enforcers.

One of the bears shifted, revealing Mano, a bear her uncle trusted. He walked over to her.

"Are you injured, Echo?" Mano scowled at the wolves. He turned his attention to her.

"No. Mindi defended me against Hyde." She sifted her fingers through Mindi's fur. She quickly summarized the story and what had happened. A sob caught in her throat as she relived the sight of Hyde's claw connecting with Mindi.

"It's going to be all right," Mano murmured. He glanced over at the bears surrounding Hyde. His features hardened when he glared at Hyde. "We will take care of him. Hyde will pay for what he has done. See to your mate."

Echo nodded, feeling somewhat comforted, but her worry for Mindi was overtaking her thoughts. She turned back to Mindi and kissed her head.

Jatix reached underneath Mindi and lifted her into his arms.

Mindi whimpered slightly.

"Be careful with her!" Echo shouted. Her chest rose and fell fast. Her bear didn't like the sound of their mate in pain. Echo was taken aback by the force of the words.

"Of course," Jatix's lips curled up in the corner into a light smile. "Believe me, I wouldn't dare harm her. But we need to hurry. She's losing a lot of blood."

"Mano, are we free to go?" the other wolf shifter asked. He was slightly shorter than Jatix but had wide shoulders and dark shaggy hair.

"Lupe, take your wolf to get help." Mano gave a nod. "We'll handle this here."

"Our alpha will want to make sure the bear is punished for harming our wolf," Lupe said.

"Don't worry. He will be," Mano growled. He turned on his heel and headed over toward the other bears.

Cursing filled the air.

The bears had all shifted back to their human form.

Even Hyde.

"That bitch broke our agreement," Hyde shouted. He moved to stand, but Vick pushed him back down.

"Call my sister a bitch again, and I'll beat your ass again," her brother threatened.

Buck, another clan enforcer, stepped in between Vick and Hyde.

"And when he's done, I'll finish what he started." Cole folded his arms in front of his massive chest.

The love for her brothers filled her heart. They had always been her protectors when they were children.

Echo stood and walked alongside Jatix.

"Get back here and face me, Echo!" Hyde hollered.

"Hyde Gillian. You are under arrest under order of the Brokenclaw Clan," Mano's firm voice cut off the screaming bear shifter. He stood in front of Hyde with the other enforcers backing him. "You will answer to your alpha for attacking his niece and her mate."

"What?" Hyde bellowed. He swung around, his bewildered eyes landing on her. "Echo! I'm sorry. You know I wasn't trying to hurt you."

Echo ignored his pitiful excuse of an apology. She bit back a smirk. He would have to answer to her uncle for attacking her. Apologizing now was not going to save him from the wrath of the alpha of the Brokenclaw Clan.

She walked into the brush, trailing the wolves. Hyde was not her problem any longer.

The laws of the clan would be followed by her

uncle. Hyde would certainly pay for what he had done.

Her uncle was a stern alpha and would show Hyde no mercy. He was fierce when it came to his family. Hyde had lost control on the wrong bear.

And from the way he was still screaming her name, he knew it.

Echo's gaze fell on Mindi's limp tail. She swallowed hard and sent a quick prayer up to the gods above that her mate would survive.

She bit her lip to keep a sob from spilling from her. She didn't want to imagine life without Mindi.

They had just found each other, and she didn't want to believe that fate would take Mindi from her. They had yet to seal the bond between them.

They exited the woods about a mile from Echo's home. Two trucks were parked on the edge of the road. By the looks of it, they had heard Mindi's call for help and immediately jumped into action.

"Here. We will put Mindi in the back of my truck." Jatix nodded to the dark pickup truck.

The other enforcer—Echo hadn't caught his name—went and opened the bed.

Jatix motioned to Echo. "You get in first. There's a couple of blankets back here. You can use one to cover yourself, and we can lay Mindi down on the other one."

Echo nodded and hopped into the bed of the truck. She hadn't thought twice about all of them being naked post shifting. She grabbed the blanket, thankful it was soft and not hard and scratchy. She wrapped it around herself then spread out the second one for him to lay Mindi on.

He gently lowered Mindi down. Echo grabbed the ends of the blanket and brought Mindi closer to her. She tugged the material over Mindi, trying to cover her.

"Make sure you hold on tight. I'll try not to go to fast." Jatix closed the tailgate and jogged to the driver's door.

The other wolves were already climbing into the second truck.

Jatix's truck engine roared to life.

Echo sighed. She leaned her head back and stared at the moon. She kept one hand on Mindi as the truck gently rocked.

Jatix guided it to the road. They drove toward

the hill that would lead them to town. She wasn't sure how the wolves had heard Mindi's howl, but she was glad they had.

Mindi whined. Echo leaned forward and brushed a hand over Mindi's fur on her head. Her eyes were still closed.

"Hold on, mate," Echo murmured. The wind coursed through her hair. The cool night air brought about goosebumps on her skin. She held the blanket against her tighter.

Within twenty minutes they had arrived at a house. A large burly man stepped from inside. She recognized him as Mindi's father, the beta of their wolf pack.

Mick rushed down the stairs and ran over to the truck. Jatix stepped out of the vehicle and came to the back.

"How is she?" Mick demanded.

Jatix opened the door and snagged the blanket Mindi rested on and tugged it toward them.

"She's still unconscious," Echo announced.

"Who did this to my daughter?" Mick snarled.

Jatix picked Mindi up and held her close to him.

"It was Hyde," Echo announced. She slipped to the edge of the truck bed and held the blanket over her. "He didn't take too kind to me breaking off our arrangement for Mindi."

"Why would you do such a thing?" He nodded to Jatix who headed toward the house.

A woman stepped from it who had to be Mindi's mother.

Echo turned her attention back to the beta. She held her head high and thrust her shoulders back. She was a proud bear and was not ashamed that her mate was a wolf.

Mindi was hers.

"Because we are destined mates." She met Mick's stare head-on. She wasn't afraid of him or his wolves. It was common knowledge that wolves were accepting of other species as mates.

Mick's features softened.

"I knew it. I could tell there was something between the two of you the night of your engagement party. Glad you girls came to your senses." He held out a hand to her.

She took it and allowed him to help her to the ground.

"Now let's get my daughter healed up. It's going to take more than a bear's claws to take Mindi out."

CHAPTER SIXTEEN

Mindi was racing through the woods. She was on a never-ending path. Her heart pounded. She turned and looked over her shoulder.

The bear was gaining on her.

His savage growl echoed behind her.

She pushed harder, trying to put more distance between them. Her four legs were eating up the path, but it would appear that no matter how fast she ran, the bear was gaining on her.

Her breath was ripped from her at the sensation of claws tearing at the flesh of her hind leg.

Mindi screamed.

She sat up and blinked. Her pulse thundered in her ears. She found herself in her old bedroom.

Her body trembled from the adrenaline coursing through her veins from the nightmare. She looked down and discovered herself dressed in a light cotton nightgown.

Her mother.

Only Adele Martin would dress her youngest child in something so girlie and frilly. Not that Mindi didn't appreciate a great skirt or dress when the occasion called for it, but this was a little bit much.

Mindi grimaced at the lace and doilies.

But seriously, this was what her mother put on her?

Mindi shook her head and pulled the nightshirt up to check out her wound. The memories of the burning sensation from Hyde's claws tearing into her was fresh.

Looking at her stomach and thigh, there was no sign of anything. A sigh of relief escaped her. Her attention was drawn to the warm body next to her. Echo was curled up in the bed.

Mindi smiled and lay next to her mate. She was unsure of what happened. The last thing she remembered was standing to let out the second distress howl. She'd moved to stand next to Echo, and that was where things had gone black.

Mindi leaned over and kissed Echo's forehead.

Her mate must have saved her.

She wasn't sure how Echo would have done it, but they were going to have a nice long talk. Mindi didn't want to think of what could have happened. Echo should not have come between her and Hyde.

"You're awake." Echo's husky voice broke the silence.

Mindi's gaze dropped back to her. A small smile played on her lips. She leaned over and touched her lips to Echo's.

They broke apart and stared at each other.

"How long have I been out?" Mindi reached up and pushed Echo's dark hair from her face.

"A little over a day." Echo slid closer to Mindi, closing the gap between them. She reached up and entwined their fingers together. "How do you feel?"

"Like a million bucks."

"Good. The healers did have to sew up the wound. His claws—" Her voice caught on a hitch. Tears welled up in Echo's eyes as they dropped down to Mindi's leg.

"It's okay. We are safe." Mindi squeezed Echo's hands. "He can't hurt us now."

"It should be me comforting you." Echo smiled, blinking back her tears. She barked a laugh and wrapped her arms around Mindi.

They lay together, in each other's embrace. Mindi breathed a sigh of relief that her mate was unharmed.

Hyde was a deranged bear, and she'd just known things would not end well. She had been ready to face death in order to make sure Echo survived.

"How did you get me to my parents' house?" Mindi glanced over at Echo. Her parents weren't close to Echo's place up in the mountains.

"Well, when you howled, the calvary came." Echo chuckled.

"Really?"

"Oh, yes. My brothers showed up and kicked Hyde's ass, and our clan's enforcers heeded the call, as did a few of your pack's enforcers," Echo said softly.

Mindi was shocked so many people had come to the rescue. She had assumed maybe one person would hear her. She was desperate at the time and just needed someone to help.

"What happened then?"

Echo recapped what Mindi had missed when

she was unconscious. She would have to thank Jatix and the enforcers. When it came to the promise of punishment of Hyde, Mindi stiffened.

"What will happen to him?" she asked.

"I'm not sure. He's in the clan's jail for the moment, waiting for the alpha to render a judgment." Echo's bottom lip quivered.

"Hey, what's wrong?" Mindi reached up and ran her thumb across the plump lip. Echo's eyes were filled with ears. She sniffed and lifted Mindi's hand. She dropped a kiss to the back of it.

"I was so scared that you would die before we could get you to the healers. You had lost so much blood, and I —"

"Shh…" Mindi gathered her tight and held her.

Echo's body trembled; her grip on Mindi was hard.

Echo exhaled and raised her head. Her bloodshot eyes met Mindi's. The horror of what she'd been through was clear in her eyes. Mindi's heart clenched, and she wished she could take it all away from her mate.

"I don't ever want to imagine what life would be like without you. When I saw all of that blood, I was scared."

"It's okay. They got me to the healers just in

time. I'm good as new." Mindi lifted the nightshirt to show there was no scar. Thanks to her shifter genes, her body had completely healed.

Echo's hand trailed softly over Mindi's stomach and down to her thigh.

A ripple of desire snuck its way through Mindi. She couldn't help it. Her mate was touching her, and her body was instantly taking notice.

Mindi covered Echo's hand with hers. She lifted it, and it was now her turn to drop a kiss to it. There was so much weighing on her heart that she had to share her feelings with Echo. If she'd learned one thing from their altercation with Hyde, it was that life was too short and she couldn't take anything for granted.

"Echo, there is something I have to tell you." She grew nervous. Her wolf snorted and sat back, watching.

"What is it, Mindi?"

Mindi stared into Echo's big dark eyes, and the butterflies in her stomach disappeared. There was nothing she couldn't tell this woman. This was who fate had determined was to be her other half, and she was prepared to spend the rest of her life with Echo.

"I love you, and my wolf wants to claim you

and your bear. You belong to me, and there is no one else for me." Mindi's vision blurred. She couldn't believe she was crying, but her emotions were getting the better of her.

"I love you, too, and my bear wants the same. She wants to make you ours forever." Echo's smile faltered for a moment. "I don't know what I would have done had something happen to you."

Mindi drew Echo to her and covered her mouth with hers. Their kiss was one of passion and love. Mindi tried to deepen it, but Echo pulled back.

"Are you crazy? You almost died yesterday. You need to rest."

"Fine." Mindi chuckled and shook her head. Even though she felt okay, she would do as her mate wished. They were going to have an eternity together.

Echo snuggled into Mindi's side. She wrapped an arm around Mindi's waist as if to protect her from an unseen enemy.

But Mindi wasn't going to complain. She was content to hold her woman in her arms. That night, she hadn't thought she'd ever do this again.

A knock sounded at the door.

"Come in," Mindi called out.

The door opened, and her parents crept into the room.

"Oh, you're awake!" her mother exclaimed. Her face lit up as she breezed toward the bed. "We didn't think you would be up yet. We were just coming to check on you and Echo to see if there was anything you needed."

"We're good, Mom." Mindi and Echo sat up in the bed and rested back against the headboard.

Adele flew to her and sat on the edge of the bed. Her amber eyes were identical to Mindi's.

"I was so worried about you. There was so much blood." Adele reached up and cupped Mindi's cheek.

"We've raised her tough," Mick grumbled. He walked over to her side of the bed. He bent down and kissed the top of her head. "I'm proud of you, Mindi. But the next time you have to face a grizzly, you run."

Laughter went around the room.

"Well, Dad. Hopefully the only one I'll be facing is the one right here." Mindi picked up Echo's hand and kissed the back of it.

"I'm so happy you found each other," Adele gushed. She patted Mindi's leg. "We honestly didn't think this one would ever settle down."

"Mom," Mindi groaned.

Adele didn't have a filter, and the moment she warmed up and got to know Echo, she'd be spilling embarrassing stories.

"What did I say?" Adele grinned. She shrugged and waved. "You must be someone special if Mindi's wolf is drawn to you."

"My bear loves being around Mindi. It was mutual," Echo said, glancing over at Mindi.

"I was thinking we could—"

"Adele, let's give this two some privacy. They don't need us hovering around them. Mindi is going to be fine. The healer said she's made a full recovery." Mick rested his hands on his waist.

"But I figured—"

"Adele." Mick tilted his head to the side, raising his eyebrows.

"Okay." Adele turned and kissed Mindi's cheek. "I love you, pumpkin."

"Love you, too, Mom." Mindi softened.

Adele was apparently overly excited that one of her children had found their mate. Mick held his hand out for his wife who took it and stood. Adele tossed a wink toward Mindi and Echo and closed the door behind her.

Finally, Mindi and Echo were alone.

"Your parents are cute." Echo giggled.

"My mother can be a little overbearing." Mindi rolled her eyes, but she truly loved her parents deeply.

"Well, she obviously cares about you and wants what is best for you."

"Oh yeah?" Mindi turned to Echo and pulled her close. She nuzzled Echo's nose with hers. "And what is best for me?"

"Me."

A growl escaped Mindi. The sweet scent of her woman was bringing her wolf to the surface. She didn't want to wait any longer.

Echo was hers to claim, and the time was now for her to take what the gods had gifted her.

Mindi leaned in and captured Echo's lips. She wasn't going to let go until Echo was officially hers.

E cho moved closer to Mindi. Her bear was pacing back and forth in anticipation of what was to come.

Echo knew without question that she was going to claim her mate.

Her heart pulsated as the need to sink her teeth

into Mindi's flesh increased. They became almost frantic removing their clothing.

Echo sighed at the feeling of Mindi's toned body pushing against hers. Mindi's hands skimmed her, sending a shiver down her spine.

Echo's body belonged to Mindi. She wasn't shy at all about her figure when she was with her.

Her mate loved her body and always ensured Echo knew it.

Mindi's mouth traveled along Echo's chin. She trailed hot, wet kisses down her neck. Mindi buried her face into the crook of Echo's shoulder. Her warm breath skated over Echo's skin.

Echo's body jerked when Mindi ran her tongue over her skin.

"Mindi," Echo gasped.

Mindi lifted her head and kissed Echo again.

Their bodies became entwined on the bed. They rolled over until Mindi was braced over Echo. Their lips were still connected while their bodies writhed against each other.

Nothing else existed in the world except them.

Echo's body was overheating. Her core clenched in anticipation. Mindi moved above her, ensuring that every aspect of their bodies touched each other.

Mindi's smaller breasts brushed Echo's.

A groan slipped from Echo. She loved the feeling of her mate's breasts moving against hers. She reached up and cupped Mindi's mounds.

Their legs parted, allowing Mindi to straddle Echo in the most intimate way they could be. They thrust against each other in rhythm, their honey-slick clits slipping over one another.

Echo gripped Mindi's ass, holding her while thrusting her hips up to meet Mindi's.

They tore their lips from each other. The only sound in the room was their rapid breathing.

Echo's gums burned and stretched to allow her fangs to descend. Her eyes zeroed in on Mindi's shoulder. The urge to sink her teeth in the meaty part was there.

Mindi's fingers threaded themselves into Echo's dark tresses. She jerked Echo's head to the side to expose her shoulder.

Echo's stomach clenched, knowing what was about to happen.

Mindi struck.

Her fangs sank deep into Echo's shoulder. The bite sent a rippling orgasm to overtake Echo. Her body tensed while the waves of her climax claimed her. Heat flooded her body, sending her through waves of ecstasy.

Mindi lifted her head. Her lips and fangs were dripping with Echo's blood.

Her amber eyes blazed at the piercing of her animal. Echo reached up and guided her face down to hers and took her lips in a deep, passionate kiss. The taste of copper filled her, but she ignored it.

Echo gripped Mindi's hair and pulled her back. They rolled until Echo was on top. Their hips continued to thrust, sending shock waves through Echo.

"Do it," Mindi whimpered.

She turned her head to the side, presenting her shoulder to Echo. A primal need surged through Echo. She widened her mouth and lowered her head, sinking her teeth into Mindi's flesh.

Her mouth filled with Mindi's blood. Mindi's body grew taut. A cry escaped her as she bellowed through her orgasm.

Echo's bear roared.

An invisible bond wrapped itself around Echo's heart.

It was the bond of mates locking in place.

Forever, Echo and Mindi would be tethered together.

Echo released Mindi and brought her lips back to Mindi's. Their movements grew urgent, and rapid. Their bodies were slick with their juices spilling. Echo rocked her pelvis harder against Mindi.

Orgasm two was rushing toward Echo. She glanced down and met Mindi's gaze, and the bond between them tightened.

They held their stare as they tumbled into their shared orgasm.

Echo's body grew weak. She fell on top of Mindi who wrapped her arms around her.

They lay together, basking in the afterglow of their claiming. Without saying a word, they licked each other's wound.

By the next day, they would be healed, and only the sign of a mating mark would be left.

Mindi tipped Echo's chin up and pressed a chaste kiss to Echo's lips.

"I love you, mate," Mindi murmured.

"I love you, too."

EPILOGUE

"You are one lucky wolf, Mindi," Kieran Murray, a journalist from a popular photography magazine, said.

Mindi stood next to him with what she knew was a wolfish grin.

"Oh, I know." She looked at the photo he was staring at.

Tonight was her latest exhibit. It was simply titled: Echo. Mindi had organized her favorite photos she'd taken of her mate, putting on a showcase.

Waves of people were stopping in to experience Mindi's event.

Familiar laughter sounded behind her. She smiled and turned, glancing over her shoulder. Her wolf whined, wanting to go to her mate.

These portraits she was sharing with the world revealed Echo as a new woman coming into her sexuality.

Echo now saw how beautiful she was and walked around the studio with confidence. A wide grin was plastered on her face as she spoke with patrons.

The show was a hit.

Echo was a star. She was the perfect model and was made to be in front of the camera. Mindi made sure she captured Echo when she could. Her sexy bear was her favorite subject.

"Are you selling any of these?" Kieran asked. He turned to Mindi and nodded to the picture he'd been assessing. "This is a front-page quality shot. Her eyes are so expressive."

"I'd have to speak it over with the model herself." Mindi chuckled. Part of the collection was up for sale tonight. There were some photos that were to remain private for only Mindi and Echo.

Mindi found her attention being pulled back to Echo.

Her mate was in an off-the-shoulder black dress that hugged her curves. Echo's hourglass figure left Mindi's mouth dry. Echo's head was held high. She wanted to wear the dress so that it would reveal her claiming mark.

A deep sense of complete satisfaction resonated inside Mindi. She had never thought she would take a mate, and now, after the past few months, she wouldn't want to have it any other way.

Echo was more than enough for her.

"Please find out. I'd love to purchase this one." He nodded to the photo. It was one of Echo sitting in a chair. In it, she wore a crisp white suit. The jacket was buttoned close but fell open to reveal Echo was shirtless. She was barefoot and stared straight ahead into the camera lens. Her dark-brown eyes were wide and captivated all who gazed upon the artwork.

"I have your contact number. I'll get back with you on it."

"Thanks."

Mindi walked away, heading toward Echo. She never could stand to be away from her for long.

Their animals always craved each other and loved spending time together out in the wild.

Mindi came up to Echo's side and wrapped her arms around her.

"I was wondering where you were, mate?" Echo gasped. She leaned into Mindi's arms and kissed her cheek. "Did you hear?"

"What, babe?"

"Every picture that we had for sale is now sold." Echo bounced in place with excitement.

"That's wonderful." Mindi leaned in and nibbled on Echo's ear. Being this close to her, she could practically forget that they were surrounded by at least a hundred people roaming through the studio.

"I was thinking." Echo turned around and faced Mindi. She raised her arms and entwined her fingers at the base of Mindi's neck, drawing them close. She popped a chaste kiss on Mindi's lips, a wicked gleam appearing in her eye. "I have an idea."

"And what might that be?" Mindi's hands skated Echo's torso and snuck around to cup her ample ass.

"I want you to star in my own personal photo shoot."

Mindi grinned. She pressed a hard kiss to Echo's mouth. She loved her mate and was never shy about showing Echo affection.

Echo belonged to her, and Mindi had no problem telling anyone. It was the wolf in her who was aggressive and possessive when it came to Echo.

After Echo's uncle had gone to the clan's council, there were many meetings about the old ancient traditions. The council recognized Echo and Mindi's mating, and last Mindi heard, the Brokenclaw Clan would be throwing out their rules of outside mating.

Her mate was a trailblazer, and she couldn't be prouder of her.

"I'm sure I can arrange something. I seem to know this amazing photographer who could teach you a few things when it comes to photography." Mindi dropped another kiss on Echo's lips. Her mate's giggle was the most beautiful sound she'd ever heard. "And I would have one stipulation."

"Oh? And what would that be?" Echo's perfectly sculpted eyebrows rose.

"You'd have to be naked when you're taking my pictures."

"Why would I be clothed?" Echo winked at her

and tried to move away, but Mindi grabbed her arm and pulled her back. This was her mate, and she couldn't get enough of her.

"One more kiss," Mindi teased her.

Echo fell back into her arms. Their lips connected in one scorching kiss.

Echo drew back and grinned at Mindi. She reached up and played with Mindi's long tresses.

"This show is over in an hour."

Mindi's grin spread wide. She glanced around her studio and took in all of their guests. Her mate was right. The show wasn't over yet.

"One hour. Then you better be upstairs in the loft, naked and waiting for me."

Echo backed away, her lips curved up in a sexy smirk. She spun around and glanced over her shoulder.

"You just better not be late, wolf."

Echo walked away into the crowd, her hips swaying seductively.

Mindi wanted to throw her head back and howl.

She had one hour until she could toss everyone out.

Then, she'd remind Echo why they belonged together.

Loving this series? The next book, Wanted by the Wolf (The Nightstar Shifters book 5) is now available!

Want to stay updated on Ariel Marie's releases, sign up for her mailing list!

LETTER FROM THE AUTHOR

Dear Reader,

Thank you for taking the time to read my book! I hope you enjoyed reading Mindi and Echo's story. I've been wanting to do another bear shifter story for a while now and Echo came to mind.

If you want me to keep this series going, say so in your review. This is how authors know readers love their books!

Love,

Ariel Marie

Wanted by the Wolf

THE NIGHTSTAR SHIFTERS BOOK 5

One scent triggers a wolf's craving. Two humans needing protection. Fate is about to intervene yet again.

Skye Lennon was on the run for her life. A civil war had recently broken out amongst the wolves and humans in her hometown. Death and violence surrounded them, making it no longer safe for her small family. Her son's father was now dead, and they were being hunted by his pack.

Howling Valley was a town deemed safe for humans.

She arrived and was welcomed with open arms by the new alpha and a certain enforcer.

Ricca Radcliff was a wolf who desired more in life. She was tired of the desk job and the steady day-to-day work. She was meant for more, so she applied and was accepted to join the elite enforcers of her pack. Defending those in need was her call- ing. After intense training, she was finally awarded her first job.

A protection detail.

Simple enough.

One whiff of the tantalizing human and her wolf immediately wanted to claim her.

Skye belonged to her.

Ricca was going to have to prove they belonged together and she could keep them safe. Even if she had to fight an entire pack alone, no one would take her woman from her.

Grab Wanted by the Wolf (The Nightstar Shifters book 5) now!

Deadly Kiss

THE IMMORTAL REIGN 1

A vampire princess. A human. One drop of blood changed their lives forever.

Vampires had taken everything from Quinn Hogan during the war. She had spent her entire life hiding from them. The last thing Quinn wanted in life was to be matched to one. Each human was required by law to enter the draft. Her name was randomly picked for submitting her blood sample.

Chances of being chosen? A million to one.

Luck had never been on her side.

Quinn matched with a vampire.

Now she was being shipped off to some random vampire who would probably bleed her dry.

Velika Riskel didn't want a mate. As the warden of Northwest America, there was no time for her to take a mate. When the human arrived, she had planned to release her, but one look into Quinn's hazel eyes and all of that changed.

Velika and Quinn's relationship was doomed from the start. Velika was a seasoned warrior who wasn't afraid of challenges. The vampire princess was determined to win Quinn's heart, defend her against a rival, and then claim her.

Don't miss this sexy, FF vampire romance tale. Grab it today!

Moon Valley Shifters

A FF WOLF SHIFTER BOXSET

Three steamy stories of female shifters finding the mate destined for them. If you love sexy as sin, F/F wolf shifters paranormal romance stories, that will leave you breathless, then grab this hot box set!

Book 1 Lyric's Mate

Lyric moved to Moon Valley for a fresh start. A new town, a new home, and a new job was a dream come true. Finding that her new boss was her mate was totally unexpected. Will she be able to keep her wolf at bay?

Book 2 Meadow's Mate

Meadow, the new teacher in town had her eyes on the only female enforcer in the pack. Little did she know, the enforcer had Meadow in her sights. When a group of rogue wolves blows into town, will Sage be able to save her?

Book 3 Tuesday's Mate

Tuesday, the new accountant in town was setting up her new business in Moon Valley. Tuesday is entranced by Sunni, the coffee shop owner. Their wolves know they are meant for each other. But will Sunni and Tuesday listen to their beasts?

WARNING: These stories are sexy, fast-paced and will leave you begging for more.

Want to hear more from this tantalizing book?
Grab it today!

ABOUT THE AUTHOR

Ariel Marie is an author who loves the paranormal, action and hot steamy romance. She combines all three in each and every one of her stories. For as long as she can remember, she has loved vampires, shifters and every creature you can think of. This even rolls over into her favorite movies. She loves a good action packed thriller! Throw a touch of the supernatural world in it and she's hooked!

For more information:
www.thearielmarie.com

Also by Ariel Marie